FUGITIVE *Heart*

MATHITU WAIRIMU

First Published in Great Britain in 2024 by
LOVE AFRICA PRESS
103 Reaver House, 12 East Street, Epsom KT17 1HX
www.loveafricapress.com[1]

---

1.   http://www.loveafricapress.com

About the Book

Makena has been living in the shadows, evading her abusive past with her young son in tow, running every time it threatens to catch up. Then she crosses paths with David, a kind-hearted stranger who thaws the icy grip of fear around her heart. She faces a dilemma she never expected—to keep running or to confront her past head-on.

As their connection deepens, Makena finds herself torn between the safety of anonymity and the hope of a future filled with love and stability. But her ex's relentless pursuit threatens to shatter the fragile peace she's found, forcing her to confront the ultimate question. Is running away truly the answer, or is it time to stand her ground and fight for the happiness she deserves?

One woman's journey to break free from her past and embrace a brighter future. Hers is a powerful story of love, courage, and second chances.

FUGITIVE *Heart*

MATHITU WAIRIMU

Chapter One

Two weeks into her new job, Makena knew her boss's son had arrived the night before, after they'd left the main house. Sometime today, she would be meeting him.

Mrs. Isabella Mutua, her boss, was diabetic and hypertensive. Makena's job was to ensure she took her medication, followed her strict dietary requirements, and had company. She couldn't complain—it earned her a nice salary and paid for her NHIF which provided her and her eight-year-old son Gerald with health insurance coverage. His school fees, at a great public school and one of the best in the country—Mrs. Mutua was friends with the headmistress and had helped Gerald get in as he had stellar grades—were the bare minimum so she was even able to save some money. She had been given a furnished two-roomed servant quarters with a half bathroom for free.

This was the best job she had gotten so far, and after being on the run with her child for a long time, she was content. And the best part was how she and Mrs. Mutua got along well and everyone loved Gerald. She didn't feel lonely or isolated as she had been feeling in the past four years.

It had been a few hard years, and after everything fell apart, she had gone through a bout of depression for months. But when it started affecting her son, she had looked for ways to cope. Her best friend, Julia, had introduced her to guided meditation and yoga which had been the most helpful. Now here she was, about as settled as she could be given the circumstances. Her diploma in social work had nabbed her this job. Her brother Charlie was friends with her boss's son, having attended university together in the US. Charlie had vouched for her, and Mrs. Mutua's daughter, Allison, had interviewed her for the position.

The son, though—he was another matter entirely.

It was a cold morning in Nairobi, so she layered Gerald with an extra jacket, and she also wore one as she walked him to school. Hopefully, she wouldn't meet that creep of Ricky today, the dad of Gerald's friend Jack, who'd accosted her the other day in his Range Rover and offered her a lift. He'd been offering way more, oblivious, it seemed, to the wedding ring on his left hand.

On her way back, she put on some Taylor Swift music; she liked her whole angry girl vibe. For months, it was all she had listened to, relating on an almost spiritual level. The music she could have written if she'd had any talent. She smiled at the thought of herself crawling out of a grave singing some 'Look what you made me do.'

She opened the door to her house, and once inside, she took off the earphones and her jacket, played a new yoga video, and got to it. When she was done, she tidied up a little, showered, and dressed in a white Safaricom T-shirt and black tights. She tied her braids in a ponytail and walked to the main house in her black Maasai sandals.

Makena performed her morning duties with her usual precision. Today, however, Mrs. Mutua had asked to have breakfast ready in the dining room so she could take it together with her son when she usually took it in bed. She'd asked her not to make him anything since he would probably have just coffee and he preferred to make it himself on the coffee maker. So she went upstairs without the usual tray. After she'd taken Mrs. Mutua's blood pressure, she collected her pills and went to wait for her in the kitchen.

She had just finished setting the table when she heard someone enter. She looked up, and the most mesmerizing eyes stared back at her. She recognized him from the photos around the house, but they didn't do him justice. He was tall, and he had to be about six-four because he was towering over her five-five frame, even from across the countertop which separated the dining room and the kitchen. His broad shoulders were covered in a short-sleeved grey hoodie which exposed a scorpion tattoo on his left bicep. He also had on black shorts and black sandals.

David Mutua was without a doubt the most attractive man she had ever seen. The thought caused her to quickly shake her head. She hadn't thought of a man in terms of his level of attractiveness in years. She couldn't. She shouldn't.

"Hi. You must be David. Welcome home. Your mother has been looking forward to your arrival."

She could have kept on rambling, but when she stopped to take a breather, he interjected.

"Hi, you must be Charlie's not-so-little sister." He joined her in the dining room, and she felt as if the room had shrunk. Before she could gather her thoughts, he stretched his hand for her to shake. "It's a pleasure to meet you Makena."

His voice was deep and inviting, and she stretched her hand to meet his. It was warm, soft, and firm. Suddenly, she was very aware of him and herself and feelings buried deep for years. He gave her a once over, and her whole body lit up at the scrutiny. It was the most intense she had ever felt.

"I see you two have met," Mrs. Mutua interrupted.

Makena pulled her hand away quickly.

"Yes, Mum, we have. Did you sleep well?" David turned his full attention to his mum, adopting a cool, calm, and collected exterior.

Makena, on the other hand, felt as if a storm was gathering within her, one she didn't care to explore. She quickly went back to setting the table and retreated to the kitchen and out to the back of the house. She would wait for half an hour for them to finish eating then go give Mrs. Mutua her medicine. By then, she would probably have gotten over her intense feeling.

She could hear David and his mother laughing. It must be great for her to have him around. Mrs. Mutua had only two children. Her husband had started a successful supermarket chain with branches all over the country. After he died, their son and daughter inherited a substantial amount of shares but hadn't taken over the business.

She thought of the last time she'd spent time with her mother. They had always been close, as she had been with her father, too, although Charlie felt like they coddled her. She'd been fourteen and in Form One of high school when her brother had gotten the scholarship. He'd gone to the US without so much as a backward glance. The entire family had been so proud of him. He was their genius, and it was finally paying up. He hadn't even had to pay for his ticket. Everyone thought he would return when he graduated, but he hadn't. He'd gotten a job and had settled down away from home.

Makena had been eighteen, just out of high school. She and her parents had been bouncing ideas on what she had to do next. Her performance in the KCSE had been average. Her best option had been a diploma. She had decided on social work because she liked taking care of people.

Before she could enrol, her parents died in an awful crash on their way home from a friend's wedding. The entire matatu they were on perished. She'd been heartbroken. It had taken two days to reach her brother and inform him. To his credit, he'd taken the first flight he could. But by then, she had already taken charge of planning the funeral. Besides, she knew more about their wishes than he did. But she'd wished he was there every step of the way.

Two days after the funeral, he was gone, leaving her to handle everything. Packing up their house was the hardest thing she had ever done. Her eyes welled at the memory of having to sell and give away her parents' stuff.

"Penny for your thoughts?" David asked, waking her from her reverie.

She blinked hard to clear the sheen of tears from her eyes and looked up. He was leaning against the door frame.

"Is this how you take care of my mum? By leaving her all alone while you daydream? I see why your brother thinks you're a mess."

"What?" she asked, infuriated, standing up and facing him. "That was unfair and uncalled for. I never leave your mother alone, and the only reason I did today is because you were there. I'm good at my job. My boss hasn't complained, so I don't care what you or my brother, who by the way hasn't known me for fifteen years, think. Excuse me while I get back to work."

Makena was so angry, she thought she was vibrating. She couldn't believe what she'd heard. On top of the fact her brother hadn't cared about her enough to want to meet his nephew or know what kind of life she was building, he'd been telling people she was a mess. Why had he recommended her for this job, then? She could imagine the conversation. Poor Charlie with his poor messed-up sister who couldn't take care of herself: *please get her a job so I don't have to deal with her.* She seriously considered quitting, but wouldn't it be proving him right?

As she gave Mrs. Mutua her medication, she couldn't decide who she was angrier at: her brother or David. At this point, she wouldn't mind using her well-acquired self-defence skills on either of them.

"Are you okay, Makena? You look rattled. Don't worry about David. I know he looks imposing, but he's a nice young man."

"I'm fine," she answered too quickly. She wanted this day to be over. She didn't want to be anywhere near David. He didn't rattle her, he infuriated her. Well, he rattled her, too, but the fury was more than the rattling.

"David is taking me out for lunch today. You can have the day off."

Gratitude was too small a word for what she felt. She went to her house and did her laundry, then spent the rest of the day watching a comedy show on her laptop. She didn't watch a lot of TV, but she felt she was owed the laughs. By the time Gerald came home from school, she was back to her usual self. She gave him his snack and helped him with his homework.

When he took his rollerblades outside, she went to the main house to prepare supper, wanting a head start because she'd decided to have supper with Gerald in their house so she would have to cook at home, too. She'd informed Gerald they would have their meals together rather than in the main house. The more she limited her interaction with David, the better it would be for her.

She set about slicing and dicing, so busy she didn't realize when she was no longer alone in the kitchen.

"I want to apologize for what I said earlier. You were right, I was unfair," David said.

Makena didn't turn around. She kept herself busy, hoping he would go away. His earthy scent was proving to be a distraction.

"I spoke to my mum, and she said that you are doing a great job taking care of her."

"You're forgiven," she said and continued preparing the ingredients for chicken breast, greens, and ugali.

David leaned on the counter and splayed his arms. She could no longer ignore him, so she looked at him.

"I met Gerald just now. He's a good kid. He was curious about my car and asked if I could take him for a drive."

This surprised her—Gerald rarely, if ever, talked to people he didn't know, especially in her absence.

"I'm sorry he bothered you. I'll ask him not to do that again." She didn't want her son to interact with David. She wanted to keep contact with him at the minimum. Gerald knew not to disclose too much about their lives to strangers, but still, keeping him away from David was more for her sake.

"I don't mind. I'm taking Allison's kids for a game drive at Nairobi National Park on Sunday. Maybe he can come with us. I'm sure he would enjoy it."

Makena stiffened. One would think he'd asked to sacrifice her son.

"No, he can't," she answered quickly. "Sunday is my day off, and we have plans."

"Okay, maybe some other time."

She nodded then went about her business cooking. David didn't leave, so she tried to ignore him. It was hard to do when she could feel his gaze following her all over the kitchen. By the time she was done, her entire being was a tightly wound coil.

She had met him all of twelve hours ago, and she was extremely attracted to him. She was even willing to admit he rattled her. She had spent years being closed off, physically and emotionally. David was threatening her doors, at least the physical ones. She couldn't deal with whatever was happening, so she chose to run.

When she was done cooking, she called Mrs. Mutua and informed her Gerald wanted something else for supper and she would be cooking in her house before she fled.

Chapter Two

Makena made fried pork, greens, and ugali for her and Gerald. He loved pork, so it was a joy watching him wipe his plate clean.

"I met Uncle Charlie's friend. He said I can call him Uncle David."

Gerald adored Charlie, which was funny because he'd never met him in person. He talked to him on the phone, and they Skyped occasionally. He also sent birthday presents and Christmas gifts to them. But he hadn't been home since before Gerald was born. It stood to reason Gerald liked David; he was the closest connection he had to his only other family.

"They went to school together," Makena said in explanation.

"Uncle David said they see each other a lot, that's probably why. He has a very nice blue car, he said it is called a Porsche. He is going to take me for a drive."

Gerald seemed completely enthralled. He liked cars and always bemoaned the fact they didn't have one. Her best friend Julia had a grey Ractis, and she always let him ride in the front with her.

"That was nice of him, but Gerald, David is busy. I don't want you bothering him. Also, remember that you shouldn't get into cars with strangers," she warned.

It was a lesson she had drilled onto him for a long time, especially since the last time he'd gotten into a car without her, she'd almost lost him. She shuddered at the memory. She couldn't imagine that happening again.

"I know, but he's a friend of Uncle Charlie, and we live in his house. He would probably bring me back, anyway."

She laughed. Gerald was right—she knew David wouldn't kidnap her son. She just didn't want him to be too close to him, that's all.

ON SUNDAY, WHILE MRS. Mutua was at church, Makena had Julia pick them up. They were going to Garden City Mall for lunch and some afternoon fun for Gerald. Julia was pregnant with her first child. She was the closest Gerald had to a godmother and had been there for Makena through everything. Makena was in the process of planning a surprise baby shower for her. During the drive, Gerald chattered about his new school and friends. He talked about David, and she just knew Julia would bring it up.

After lunch, Gerald went to the park to play, and they sat nearby to watch over him and chat.

"How are you doing? Are you over the street smokies phase?"

Julia was in her seventh month of pregnancy and had been craving street-made smokies for weeks.

"We're over that now. This week, we're crazy for pineapples. Henry is having a hard time with this one. The mere thought of pineapples drives him crazy. I used to hate them, too, but Joy gets whatever she wants," Julia said, cradling her baby bump.

"Joy? No, we're not naming her Joy. She can have Olive. I don't use it, anyway."

Julia had been floating baby names through her since she found out she was having a girl. Makena kept trying to convince her to name her baby Olive, which was her first name. She hadn't used it in four years, not since she'd left Paul, Gerald's father.

"If I name my child after you, Henry will leave me."

They laughed at the jab. Henry and Julia were the most functional couple Makena had ever seen after her parents. They loved each other, and they had been together for five years, married for three. Julia had wanted to wait until she was done with her master's degree and her career as an IGCSE teacher took off before they started a family. Henry had supported her decision, and now, they were expecting their first child, a girl. Makena couldn't be happier for her friend.

"We both know he would never survive without you," she said.

"We'll never find out now, will we?"

They laughed, and Makena believed this with all her heart.

"How are you guys really, sweetie?" Julia asked with seriousness. She wanted the real answer, and she was the only person Makena trusted enough to give it to. Julia was more than her friend—she was her sister.

"Gerald is his usual self, thriving despite everything, and I'm just there, I guess," she said.

Makena had always been in awe of her son. He took every challenge in stride, and he rarely faltered. She had worried about the impact of her disastrous relationship with his father on him. She'd even gone to a child counsellor, and after a few sessions, the woman had assured her her son was okay.

"What do you mean?" Julia asked.

"I love my job, and my boss is this great woman who treats us well. She gave us a nice house to live in for free and even got Gerald into that school."

"All those are good things, but you don't sound thrilled. What's the problem?"

"The problem is that I have resigned myself to the fact I'll never stop running. Sooner or later, Paul will find us again, and we will have to run again. When does it stop? Gerald is young now and maybe even sees all this as some sort of adventure, but what about when he gets older? How will I explain to him that we can't stop because his father will never stop looking for us?" Her eyes welled up.

"Sweetie, I told you that if you ever decide to go after him, I will help you in any way you need," Julia said, taking her hand in hers.

"I know, but I can't ask that of you. I can't put you in this kind of danger. You're pregnant, and you have a family of your own. You know what he's capable of."

"I do, and I'm so proud of you. You dared to leave him, and look how well you have done with Gerald. But sweetie, it's okay to take a breather. You can stop and enjoy the moment, it's allowed."

Makena sighed. Julia was right, but she didn't know how to stop. And sometimes, she thought she had forgotten how to enjoy life.

Julia drove them home a few hours later. Just as she was driving off, David stopped his car next to them outside the gate. He honked so the gateman could open the gate and rolled down the window.

"Hi, Gerald, Makena. How was your day?"

Makena said hi back.

"It was great, Uncle David. We went to the mall with Aunt Julia. I had a milkshake and a lot of chips. I rode a quad bike and played on the bouncing castles," Gerald said excitedly.

"That sounds great. Maybe next time, you can come with my niece and nephew and me to the park. We had a good time, too."

Makena looked up at him, and their eyes met. Butterflies fluttered in her stomach, and a warmth filled her. David was smiling at her. He bit his lower lip, and she darted her eyes and fidgeted with her keys.

"Can we, Mum? Can we go to the park?" Gerald asked, tugging at her hand and breaking the moment.

"I don't know, Gerald, maybe," she replied, turning her attention back to her son.

"I have to go now. I have a hot date tonight," David said.

As he drove into the open gate, Gerald asked Makena what a hot date was.

Argh, this man! How was she going to explain this to her son?

A FEW DAYS LATER, MAKENA and Gerald were leaving to go to school, and David was going out for his run. He stopped to greet them as she closed the door.

"Good morning, Gerald. You off to school?" he greeted, pulling his earphones from his ears.

"Yeah, my mum walks me every day even though I told her she doesn't have to but she does this all the time," Gerald responded grumpily.

Makena turned to face them.

"I like walking you to school," she protested. "Morning, David."

"Hi, Makena. Maybe I can walk with you guys. Then it won't just be you and your mum."

"There's nothing wrong with a mother walking her son to school, thank you very much."

However, it didn't stop David from joining them as they headed to Gerald's school. Both of them let the boy's chatter occupy the walk, only chiming in when he asked them a question.

"How are you liking working for my mother?" David asked on their way back.

"It's great. It's my first home care job. Your mum is nice, and she treats Gerald like her grandson, which is amazing."

"My mum is great like that. She likes you, too. I misjudged you when I met you. But in my defence, I only knew what your brother told me about you."

"I guess you're right." Then she paused for a second. "Does Charlie think I'm a mess?"

"He loves you."

Makena sighed. She didn't blame him. She hadn't told him why she'd left Paul, just that things hadn't worked out. She also realized that although she'd reduced asking for his help to a minimum, she *had* asked several times since she'd left Paul. He also knew she moved a lot and kept changing jobs.

"What do you do when you're not working?" David asked.

They were almost home.

"I take care of my son," she answered. "There's no leave of absence when you're a mother."

"What about his dad, does he help? Or take him sometimes?"

She stopped and looked at him.

"Gerald is my son. Taking care of him is my responsibility and mine alone. Have a nice day."

She quickly walked inside the gate and headed for her house, leaving David stunned.

"Wait," he said, catching up to her fast. He held her shoulder and turned her around to face him. "I'm sorry. I just want to get to know you."

She looked at him. She had been opening up to him. She enjoyed talking to him. It wasn't his fault she saw red whenever someone mentioned Paul. He had no idea what she had been through. She would never tell him or anyone else because it meant reliving the worst years of her life.

"Gerald's father is not in the picture. He hasn't been in the picture since we separated. I just don't like talking about him. Thank you for walking us to school. Gerald had fun."

"I had fun, too. He's a nice kid."

She opened the door and turned around to excuse herself.

"Are you going in for some yoga?"

"What? How did you know?" she asked, surprised.

"I've seen you through the window. You have some impressive moves," he said nonchalantly.

"Were you peeping? You're a Peeping Tom," she said in mock outrage.

"I wasn't peeping. I saw you and couldn't help but look. Unlike your window, there are no curtains on my eyes."

"I will make sure to close the curtains in the future," she said with a laugh.

"Well, not on my account. I enjoyed the show." He winked.

She pulled at her braids, and as he took a step towards her, she saw what was going to happen clearly. He was going to put his hand on the door frame beside her. Then he was going to lean in and kiss her, probably on the lips. She took a step back inside the door.

"I have to go do my thing now. Your mum will be up soon, and I need to start working."

There was no more effective mood killer than her mentioning his mother. She closed the door and leaned against it, hearing David swear and walk off.

As she did her yoga, all she kept hearing was a voice in her head uttering, 'This is bad' over and over again. Being intensely attracted to her boss's son and her brother's best friend was the last thing she wanted. She couldn't allow that to happen.

Chapter Three

If there was something Makena's past had given her in abundance, it was a sense of self-preservation. She was what one would call paranoid, but all she wanted was to ensure the past never caught up with her or repeated itself.

David wasn't the first man she had felt stirrings for since she'd left Paul. But she never left room for such feelings to grow, nipping them in the bud through extreme avoidance. The only person she had ever opened herself to was Paul—how tragically this ended.

With David, avoidance was going to be harder than she'd imagined. She worked for his mother and lived in the same compound with him. Gerald loved him—David was attentive to him, played with him, and sometimes, even helped him with his homework. Makena didn't know how to tell her son he couldn't bond with him. She'd never had to since Gerald was as cautious as she was in letting people in. She'd tried hard not to spread her paranoia over to her son, but when someone you trusted failed you so spectacularly, no matter your age, it was bound to give you trust issues.

She didn't remember the last time she'd read so much or exercised as much as she had in the past few days. Where earlier, she'd liked how her job was so freeing, she now resented the fact she had too many hours with nothing to do.

It was a blessed relief when Julia came to visit her one afternoon on her day off. She talked about how much she loved Makena's house. Makena had made her some chicken which she loved. They talked about Julia's most recent doctor's visit. Her baby was doing great, and she couldn't wait for Makena to see her ultrasound photos.

"Now, tell me about this David Gerald can't stop talking about."

"When did he talk about him?" Makena protested.

"When we went to Garden City, he tells me things."

"There's nothing to tell. David is Mrs. Mutua's son. He is the one I told you about, Charlie's friend who got me the job. Gerald likes him because he drives a Porsche and knows his uncle." She tried to be as offhanded as she could.

"I'm sure there's more, like, is he married? Young? Handsome? I would assume he is Charlie's age."

"He is Charlie's age, and I will admit he is attractive. As far as I know, he is not married." Before Julia could get a word in, she added, "But all that doesn't matter. You know how I feel about relationships and men in general. I can't set myself up for that kind of hurt. Plus, it's not just me. My son doesn't need the trouble."

Makena had managed to avoid any significant interaction with David for days. She knew not to set herself up for a compromising situation. So far, she had been successful. She intended to keep avoiding him until this attraction had run its course or he left. According to his mother, he usually stayed two weeks or a month at most. She and Gerald had been having their meals in their house. Mrs. Mutua had complained about not seeing Gerald, but Makena had told her she wanted to give her privacy with her son.

"No one is asking you to marry the guy. Maybe just have some fun, of the adult kind," Julia said with a chuckle.

Makena refused to acknowledge what she had said and sipped her juice.

"I mean, I'm seven months pregnant, and I'm having some of the greatest sex of my life."

"Julia!" Makena wasn't surprised by her friend's open-book policy on her sex life. She didn't want to think of any kind of adult fun with David. If she did, she would probably never stop.

"You're a mum, but you're also a woman who has been single for four years. I would recommend sex or even a relationship. It's time, and you don't just need one, you deserve it. It doesn't have to be David. Just stop running in the other direction when the opportunity presents itself. There are good men out there. Paul was an anomaly." Julia said earnestly.

Makena didn't know what to say. She knew in her heart it was true, but she couldn't stand taking the risk of it being a mistake.

"I'll get going. Thanks for the lunch."

Makena stood up to walk her to her car, which was parked outside her house. Just as Julia was getting in, the gate opened, and David drove in with his mother in her white Subaru Outback. He stopped beside Julia's car, and they both got out.

"Hello, Mama Allison. David," Makena greeted. "This is my friend Julia."

They all shook hands and said their hellos. Mrs. Mutua seemed delighted to meet her. It was probably a surprise to her that Makena had friends since she never spoke of any. She invited them into the main house for tea, but Julia declined since she had to get home. She walked to the main house, and David got back into the car to park it.

"That's David? Wow," Julia said.

"You're married," Makena said in mock outrage.

"Yeah, but I can look. You, on the other hand, can do much more," Julia said with a wink.

Makena gasped at her audacity.

"Get out of here," she joked.

Julia laughed and drove away.

LATER, MAKENA WENT to make Mrs. Mutua her supper. It was Friday night, so she let Gerald watch TV instead of doing his homework, which he usually tackled on Saturday morning. He was watching some superhero animation on the TV in the living room. David walked into the kitchen, a shift in the air around her alerting her to his presence.

"Julia seems nice," he said as he leaned against the kitchen counter as he usually did. "How long have you been friends?"

"She's the first friend I ever made when I got into nursery school, so about twenty-five years," she answered.

"That's nice. Such friendship is hard to come by."

Then, as she stirred the rice, he took over cutting the onions and carrots for the stew.

"You're good at that. I wouldn't have thought you would know how to hold anything in the kitchen," she said, watching him in fascination.

"You wound me," he said with a chuckle. "I have lived alone for fifteen years. I had to learn my way around."

"That's a long time. After my parents died and my brother left, I was alone for a year, and it was torture. I had school and spent some time with Julia, but when I was alone, it used to get so overwhelming. I would wake up in the middle of the night and start sobbing."

David stopped and took her hand.

"I'm sorry you had to go through that alone," he said, gently squeezing her hand.

She pulled away.

"It was a long time ago. Now, I'm guaranteed company for about ten years. The only reason I got myself a kid," she said with a laugh.

"You always pull away just when you're about to let me in," David said.

She didn't know how to respond, but she didn't have to say anything because he continued.

"I'm attracted to you, you know that. And I like you."

"You can't. This is not some low self-esteem talking. I have more baggage than is okay to shoulder on someone else."

"Wow, I hope Gerald didn't hear you call him baggage."

"Not Gerald. Gerald is the light of my life. It's everything else."

"We all have a few failed relationships under our belts. Besides, Makena, you don't get to tell me whether I can like you or not. Hell, I can't tell myself not to get attracted to you. I don't know how you think you'll succeed where I failed," he said nonchalantly.

"Well, I can tell you it's not going to happen. Besides, when you first met me, you had some strong opinions about my work ethic and me as a person. What has changed?"

"I got to know you. You're a wonderful mother, and you're great at your job. And I'm overwhelmingly attracted to you because I don't believe I have met a more beautiful woman. I have observed you for weeks and never once have you put a foot wrong."

Her breath hitched, and she felt her resolve weaken as he stepped closer. She took a step back.

"I can't, David. I'm sorry," she said in a whisper.

"Fine, I'll take your word for it, but I know that you need a friend, and I can be that for you."

"One can never have too many friends. I would appreciate an even two," she answered.

BEING DAVID'S FRIEND turned out to be a wonderful thing. He was extremely attentive, but he never attempted to cross any boundaries. In the morning, after his run, he would drop by to see if he could walk Gerald to school. Sometimes, Makena just let him. They would then have tea together before she went to work. He had told her he'd decided to extend his stay a little longer.

His mother said she was hoping he decided to stay for good and settle down. She then started waxing lyrical about additional grandchildren. Makena laughed as she gave the woman her evening medication. Parents loved grandchildren—she already doted on Allison's two children, but it didn't stop her from wanting more grandkids.

It was one of the things she felt sad about Gerald missing. Paul's parents had been awed by having a grandson, but the awe had worn off soon after. Makena knew how thrilled her parents would have been by Gerald. Although she would never admit it out loud, she was sad about being the only family Gerald had.

A COUPLE OF WEEKS LATER, she and David were jogging together after they'd walked Gerald to school when a car pulled up beside them. It was Ricky. It had been a while since Makena had encountered him. He honked, and they couldn't ignore him without it looking weird.

"Hi Mama Gerald. How's it going?" he greeted.

"Hi," she responded. David cleared his throat beside her as if she could ignore his presence. "This is David."

Ricky stretched his arm from the car window, and David shook it.

"David, Ricky's son Jack is Gerald's classmate," she added.

"I've heard of him from Gerald. They seem to be close," David said.

"Are you two together? Jack says Gerald hasn't had a father in years," Ricky said.

Makena was embarrassed by the announcement. She hated that Gerald had had this conversation with other kids. It meant the issue of dads must have been brought up and he was left out. The fact Ricky had brought it up in front of David was meant to be a slap in the face for her ignoring him.

"No, we're just friends. I work for his mum," she answered.

"That's good. It means I can take you out for *nyama choma* and more over the weekend," he said.

Makena felt David withdraw, and when she turned to look, he was jogging home.

"Look, Ricky, aside from the fact that I'm not interested, there is the fact you are married. I would appreciate it if you didn't accost me again. It makes me uncomfortable and is disrespectful to your family," she said firmly.

She then took off after David. Ricky had been issuing invitations for a while. She had been dodging them, but it wasn't working. She hoped this firm rejection of his advances would do the trick.

Chapter Four

That weekend, Allison invited Makena and Gerald to her daughter's birthday party. Allison's kids were a bit younger than Gerald. The daughter, Gianna, was turning six years old, and her son Nathan was almost four. Gerald liked the kids and spent time with them when they visited their grandmother.

They dressed up and waited for David. He was driving them, along with Mrs. Mutua, to the party. David knocked on the door, and Gerald ran past Makena to open it.

"Uncle David, can we leave now?" he asked excitedly.

"Yes, we can. Please go wait in the car, the doors are open."

Gerald dashed out, and David walked inside. He had never been inside the staff apartment. Makena was suddenly aware of how small it must seem to him. She was also aware of the fact there wasn't a lot of space between them.

"Hi, David" she greeted.

"Hello, Makena. You look beautiful," he said, giving her a once-over that sent a fire throughout her body.

She was dressed in a midnight blue jumpsuit and red wedges. She had on light makeup, including some dark maroon lipstick and small gold loops. She had never been in a situation where a look had her wanting to abandon everything she believed in and take whatever she wanted.

"Thank you. So do you." When he chuckled, she added, "I mean, you look handsome."

"Well, I try. Much as I hate to interrupt whatever is going on in your mind because I like it, we have to get going."

She grabbed the gift they had gotten for Gianna, closed the door, and headed to the car. They were taking his mum's vehicle. Mrs. Mutua was in the backseat, giving Makena no other choice but to sit on the passenger seat next to David. Mrs. Mutua engaged Gerald in a conversation so Makena was free to do the same with David.

"Nice car," she said, looking at the interiors.

"It is." David then launched into describing the car's features. Somewhere along engine power, he must've realized he'd lost her. "This doesn't bode well for my efforts."

These words shook her from her reverie.

"What? What efforts?" she asked.

"My efforts to be your best friend. That can't happen if I'm boring you with drivel about cars."

"That's not entirely your fault. I know nothing about cars, and my interest in them only goes as far as their ability to take me from Point A to Point B."

"Never mind that, then. Would you like some music? As reparations for boring you, I will give you the chance to choose what we listen to," David said, fiddling with the car's radio.

"Some RnB would be nice."

A short while later, Mariah Carey's voice filled the car.

"Were you and Allison always close?" she asked after a long silence.

"Yeah, we're close in age so we've always been in the same age group. When we were little, we used to have a joint birthday party. It gave Mum such a headache to plan because she had to cater to both our interests. Fortunately, Allison was a bit of a tomboy so we weren't that different."

"Allison, a tomboy? You couldn't tell looking at her now."

David and his mum laughed and nodded in agreement.

"She completely ruined what I had in mind about having a daughter. I thought we'd be matching outfits and having tea parties only for her to borrow her brother's clothes and pick toy trucks at the supermarket," Mrs. Mutua chimed in.

"It's probably not a coincidence that Nathan and Gianna are so close in age. She ensures they have a nice relationship like the one we had," David said.

While Makena and Charles hadn't had as close a relationship, she still loved having a brother. Mrs. Mutua chipped in with some anecdotes about how naughty David was. He and his friends used to play cruel tricks on his sister.

They arrived at Allison's house in Thindigua. It was nested in a large compound which, at that moment, had been transformed into every child's dream. There was a bouncing castle, a kiddy pool, and all sorts of toys. A clown was making animal balloons and painting the kids' faces. There was a stand for food and snacks and a table for the presents.

As soon as the car stopped and the doors unlocked, Gerald jumped out. Makena barely had time to tell him to be careful.

She put the present on the table—a *Moana* sticker kit and two handwritten cards from both of them. David and Mrs. Mutua also dropped their presents. Allison joined them and called the kids to say hi. She then invited them into the house to join the adults. The children were being chaperoned by a host of staff.

Makena and David followed Allison to the house, and Mrs. Mutua opted to stay outside. Makena was introduced to the group which consisted of a few of Allison's neighbours and colleagues and her husband, James. Most of them had already met David. A buffet sat on the table in the dining room.

Makena sat on the empty two-seater couch, and David went to get the food. He thoughtfully brought a plate with just the right selection for her: a piece of chicken, vegetable salad, and pilau. He'd also brought her a glass of fruit juice. They ate quietly, occasionally joining in the ongoing conversation.

Just as they were finishing up, Caitlin arrived. She was Allison's best friend and Gianna's godmother. She was also David's on-again-off-again girlfriend, according to his mother who didn't seem to like her. Caitlin ignored all the other guests and went straight for David, giving Makena a once-over then completely disregarded her.

"Hi, baby, it's been a while. Where have you been?" she asked, leaning down to hug him and in the process putting her full bosom on display. She wore a red figure-hugging number showing ample cleavage.

"Hi, Cait. I've been busy." David returned the hug.

Caitlin perched herself on the armrest and draped a hand on David's shoulder. Having asserted her dominance over him, she turned her attention to Makena.

"David, care to introduce me to your friend?"

"Yeah, this is Makena. She is Mum's caregiver, and her son is Gianna and Nathan's friend."

Makena felt the sting of being lumped with the help. It wouldn't have stung if it had come from anyone else, but her feelings for David got the better of her. She quickly recovered when Caitlin extended her hand in greeting.

"I'm Gianna's godmother and Allison's best friend. My friends call me Cait. You can call me Caitlin."

Makena was taken aback by the condescending tone. Allison and David eyed Caitlin sharply.

"I'm kidding," she added. "Only David calls me Cait. I tried to stop him, but I like him too much."

"Caitlin, Makena is like family, and my mum thinks of her son as one of her grandchildren," Allison said.

Caitlin checked out of the conversation and, instead, turned all her attention onto David. He didn't seem that bothered by any of it. She placed her legs between his thighs and kept touching him at any opportunity.

Makena felt uncomfortable, more so because she was seated next to them. She stood up abruptly, picked up her plate and David's, and took them to the kitchen. She slipped out through the back door and joined Mrs. Mutua in the small tent next to the playground.

"Are you enjoying yourself?" Mrs. Mutua asked, oblivious of her inner turmoil.

Makena nodded, clenching at her hands to tamper down her anger, although she was convinced it was more jealousy than anger.

"Yeah, Allison is a great hostess, and her friends are nice," she answered. "Have you seen my little rascal? I was hoping to get a photo or two in."

"He's in the bouncing castle. He seems very popular. Gianna has introduced him to all her friends," Mrs. Mutua said as she pointed at the bouncing castle where Makena glanced just in time to see Gerald's head through the mesh window as he jumped. "He's a nice boy. Whatever happened to lead you two in my life, I'm glad you're here."

"We're so happy to be here. You're a nice boss when you aren't being stubborn about hydrating."

They both laughed.

Makena liked the easy camaraderie between them. It could be because she had never worked as a home caregiver before, but she had such a close relationship with Mrs. Mutua. The closest to a parental figure she had ever allowed herself since her parents died.

From the very beginning, Mrs. Mutua had insisted she didn't need a babysitter. Makena was her first caregiver—she just needed someone to remind her to take her medicines and eat well. Which was exactly what Makena did. She didn't impose onto her space, but she was there when needed. Mrs. Mutua loved Gerald, and sometimes, he called her grandma. Since she didn't live with any of her grandchildren, Mrs. Mutua liked to spoil Gerald. It was always within reason because Makena refused to let her son be spoiled into a brat, but she liked how Gerald had a grandma. This was the only job she hoped did not come to an end. She was taking great pains to ensure this wouldn't happen.

Allison soon joined them with a glass of fresh orange juice for each of them.

"I'm sorry about Caitlin. She can be obsessive sometimes," she said.

"Caitlin is here?" Mrs. Mutua asked with a groan. "I still don't know why you named her Gianna's godmother. You have better friends, Allison."

"It was six years ago. I was young and pregnant. Plus she planned my baby shower. Also, Mum, she's a good friend, and you should see her with Gianna. She is great with her," Allison defended.

Makena looked on uncomfortably.

"Well, at least you made the right choice in a husband and father of your children. I can't say the same," she said.

They both looked at her with concern, but she laughed it off.

The kids ran to them. Gianna loved Makena and thought of her as her cool aunt. When she spent the night at her grandmother's, Makena babysat. She would make all the kids popcorn and find them a nice movie to watch. She knew Gianna might feel outnumbered by the boys, but she always found a way to keep the peace by finding something all the kids liked.

"Do you want to bounce, Mum?" Gerald asked, grabbing her hand. Gianna grabbed her other hand to lead her to the bouncing castle.

Makena didn't like them. They made her feel claustrophobic. But there was a trampoline, and she compromised.

"No, honey, but we can go jump on the trampoline."

The kids nodded enthusiastically, and she allowed herself to be led away.

THE AFTERNOON GAVE way to early evening, and it was time to cut the cake, a red velvet cake with Elsa from *Frozen* laid atop in her blue gown. Gianna cut the cake as the cameraman snapped several shots. She fed her parents and brother a piece. In a playful gesture, very much unlike her serious outlook, Allison smeared cream on her daughter's face. When they were done sharing the cake, the party started wrapping up.

Mrs. Mutua wanted to leave soon after, and Makena started to join her. She resisted, having Allison's driver take her home, opting not to take David out of the party. She further insisted that Makena stay because Gerald was still playing with the other kids.

When night came, the children moved into the house, and the adults took over the outdoor space. There was music playing, and the snacks table had been replaced with drinks. David was driving them home so he didn't drink. Makena rarely indulged in alcohol; nevertheless, she gave in to a glass of wine.

As the night wore on and people got more drunk, Caitlin got more blatant in her advances on David. Makena had observed her take just two drinks—she wasn't that drunk. But it didn't stop her from grabbing David's face and trying, albeit unsuccessfully, to get a kiss in as they danced. She ground her body on his as John DeMatthew crooned one of his famous love songs on the speakers. Allison and her husband were also on the dancefloor, holding each other close.

Aside from the rising feeling of dislike for Caitlin, fuelled by jealousy, this had been a good day for Makena. She was happy about how much fun they had. She had been giddy with excitement jumping on the trampoline. While being a mum made you grow up in many ways, it also meant tapping into your inner child time and again.

At around eleven p.m., she asked David, who was no longer attached to Caitlin, whether they could leave. He signalled Allison to join them. Most of the people had left.

"We need to get going," he said.

"That's okay. Makena, do you mind if Gerald spends the night? He fell asleep, and the maid put him in the extra bed in Nathan's bedroom."

Makena was surprised. She had popped in about an hour earlier, and Gerald had been engrossed in some cartoon. She was about to say no, but she gave it some thought. If she insisted on waking him up and driving him forty-five minutes, then waking him up again to put him to bed, his night would be so disrupted. Allison's place was nice, and it wasn't like he would be amongst strangers. She agreed to the idea, and Alison promised to bring him home the next day.

This meant Makena and David would be making the drive home on their own. It would be the most time they had spent alone since the fateful run-in with Ricky. They said goodbye and walked to the car. As David drove away, Allison waved them off.

"As an act of mercy, because I know how nervous you are about leaving Gerald, I will once again let you choose the music," David said as they got into the road.

She picked the same playlist they had been listening to earlier and turned the volume low.

They drove in silence for a while, and then he broke the silence.

"So, Jack's father Ricky, what's going on there?"

Makena stayed silent for several seconds.

"Ricky is a married sleazebag who has been hitting on me from the day we met. I didn't ask for his attention, and I don't like it," she answered hotly.

"I'm sorry. It must be hard dealing with that, especially with Jack and Gerald being close." He took her hand in his.

"It's not. I just avoid him. I'm good at that."

"Don't I know it. I told you I liked you, and you shut me out even though we live in the same compound."

"I like you, too, but this is not something I can get into right now. Besides, there's always Caitlin. She seemed pretty interested."

"I'm not interested in her. We've been together, but not for a long time. I'm interested in you. You say this is not something you can get into right now, but doesn't that mean you aren't giving me enough credit? I will take this at your pace, I will not rush you, I won't ask for anything you aren't ready to give. If what you need is friendship, then I will continue to be your friend."

She squeezed his hand.

"I know this, and I appreciate it, but when you first got here, you thought I was a mess and so is my life. While that was not a legitimate analysis, it's not so far off the mark. I don't want to string you along and then abandon you at a moment's notice. I already have enough to worry about. I have been dragging my son around this country for years."

"Why do you move so much?"

Her first instinct was to go off on him, but she knew he meant no harm.

"It's for work," she answered in a tone that didn't invite further questions.

David knew not to push.

As the car pulled to a stop in traffic, she turned to look at him. She'd meant for it to be a stealing glance, but he did the same, and their eyes met. She felt heat rise from the core of her being under his gaze. She became aware of his thumb drawing circles on her wrist, and the electricity between their skins sizzled.

He bit his lower lip, drawing her attention to his mouth, then brought her hand to it and kissed the back of it.

They were brought out of their world when the car behind them honked, reminding them they were on the road.

A few kilometres from home, he pulled over at a petrol station which had a twenty-four-hour shop. He left the attendant filling up the car and went to the shop. He was in and out in a few minutes with a bottle of water. He put it in the cupholder and drove the rest of the way.

It was almost midnight when they got home. David parked the car, and they got off. He walked her to the door, where she fumbled for her keys in her small purse and finally pulled them out. She opened the door and stepped in, then she turned around.

She'd meant to say goodnight and close the door, because, surely, anything other than that would be rash and irresponsible.

Instead, she stretched out her hand and asked,

"Do you want to come in?"

Chapter Five

The pause was so long, Makena thought she had misread the whole situation. She was about to rescind the invitation when David took her hand and stepped inside. He locked the door without letting go of her hand and dropped the keys on the TV stand just next to the door.

He looked into her eyes and asked, "Are you sure?"

She had never been so sure of anything, but his intense scrutiny stole the voice from her, so all she could do was nod.

He did not need any more urging, and he led her to the bedroom, where he turned on the light, as if wanting to see all of her.

He leaned in to kiss her, and as his soft lips touched her own, everything else disappeared. All her thoughts flew out of the window. He tasted of desire, all masculine and all-encompassing. He pulled her closer in his embrace, and she gave in to the intoxicating feeling of being in his arms. Then he stepped back and turned her around. She was puzzled, but only for a moment as he pulled down the zipper on her jumpsuit.

He bared her shoulders, then slowly pulled it down past the sensuous curve of her hips. She stepped out of it and turned around to face him.

"You looked so beautiful today. When you were jumping on the trampoline, I was transfixed," he said roughly.

He looked her up and down, slowly and deliberately. It felt like hours for her, but it was mere seconds. She panted heavily, her breasts, still encased in a black bra, heaving up and down with each breath. She longed for him to come to her or pull her to him, but he wasn't going to be hurried, it seemed. As she saw the desire in his dark eyes, all her insecurities melted away. She knew without a doubt he wanted her.

So, she took a step to him, tiptoed, and linked her hands around his neck. Their lips touched in another kiss, and it was like coming home.

He let her lead, and she pulled his jacket from his shoulders then set about unbuttoning his shirt. *He is beautiful*, she thought as she exposed his chest, running her hands on the hairs there.

He stopped her as she went southward, unhooked her bra, and pulled it off, freeing her breasts. Then he laid her on her striped black and white duvet. He pulled down her panties and proceeded to make love to her with his mouth. He cupped one breast and ran his thumb on the dark nipple as he sucked erotically on the tip of the other, then alternated.

He went down on her, opening her up to a whole new world. She opened up like a flower for his tongue, dewy with moisture. As he ran his tongue on the bundle of nerves on the core of her, he slipped a finger into her.

By then, Makena had been reduced to a mass of yearning. She wanted—what, exactly, she didn't know, but she knew it was within reach. It was like looking up into a starry night and wanting to be amongst the brightness of the stars. She breathed fast and heavy as he did not miss a bit. His ministrations reached into the deepest part of her. And then, after what felt like hours, she was amongst the stars, in their brightness, their beautiful glow. It was a feeling so foreign to her, she thought it would consume her completely.

In the afterglow, he pulled away from her and pulled down his pants and boxer briefs in one swoop. Makena looked at him. He was hard, almost painfully so. She stood up on shaky legs and reached for him. He gave in to her, standing before her in all his beautiful glory. She laid him on the bed and straddled him. He handed her a condom. She ripped the foil packet and put it on him. Then she lowered herself on him, taking charge of their lovemaking, relishing the control she had over him.

She took it slow at first, teasing him, watching him, listening to his impatient grunts. She wanted this to last, and she was going to make it last, for both of them. She made love to him, long and slow, until he turned the tables on her and took charge again. Just as the awesome feeling took over her once again, he emptied into her and collapsed beside her.

They both lay there, for long minutes. Then he took care of the protection, and they slipped under the covers where he pulled her to him. For a long while, they lay in each other's arms in silence, the only sound in the room their heavy breathing.

David spoke first.

"Well, you blew my mind," he said, then kissed the back of her hand.

"The feeling is mutual," she responded.

Makena had lost her virginity to a clumsy encounter with a short-term boyfriend. Then, she had been with Paul for years. From the beginning, he had been selfish when it came to sex. It should have been a red flag had she known better, but she hadn't. She'd thought it was supposed to be like that, with nothing in it for her—maybe she just wasn't wired to enjoy sex like other women. This was what she thought whenever Julia talked about having great sex.

"I can hear the wheels of your head turning. Tell me, what are you thinking?" David asked, running his hand through her hair.

"I'm thinking that letting you into my bed was a great decision," she said, then she turned and gave him a quick kiss on the lips.

"I'm glad you think so because I plan on frequenting it as often as you'll let me. This can't be a one-time thing for me."

"I don't want it to be a one-time thing, either, David, but—"

He cut her off by placing his finger on her lips.

"Shhh. No buts, Makena. Now, we sleep."

She didn't object. Instead, a few minutes later, she started feeling drowsy. Her current replete state was a recipe for a sound night's sleep.

WHEN SHE WOKE UP THE next morning, she had a moment of panic, thinking she was back where she had run from years earlier. Only Gerald, when he was much younger, had ever been in her bed for years. It had been a shock in her system not to wake up alone, which lasted for a moment, and then memories of the previous night flooded. And she knew it couldn't be Paul.

She touched her lips where David had kissed her. She felt delicious aches where he had been inside her. Before she allowed herself to be consumed by the memories, she got out of bed, careful not to wake the man sleeping beside her. She checked her phone—no calls from Allison, so Gerald was okay. There was a text from Julia checking in on her. She updated the group she'd created for her baby shower on WhatsApp. After brushing her teeth and dressing in sweats and a T-shirt, she went to give her boss her breakfast all while pretending she hadn't spent the night in her son's arms.

When she came back to her house, David was awake and dressed, seated on the couch.

"I woke up alone in a strange bed. That was not nice of you," he said, then kissed her deeply.

"You looked so peaceful asleep, I didn't want to wake you, and I needed to feed my boss her breakfast before I start on my day off," she answered.

"Did my mother sleep well?" David asked, taking a step away from her as if he'd remembered the illicit nature of their affair.

"She did. She asked what time we came home. Don't worry, she doesn't know we spent half the night doing...you know."

He laughed and stepped close to her again.

"Wow, you can't even say it, can you? Where is the bold woman of yesternight? Don't worry, I know you wouldn't tell my mum that you spent half the night having mind-blowing sex with her son." He laid a tender kiss on her neck. "Why don't you make it up to me for leaving me alone in your bed without a word?"

"I brought breakfast. I made some extra toast." She pointed at the plate on the TV stand. She didn't even remember putting it there. Her senses were consumed by David.

"I'm not hungry for food."

He kissed her passionately and led her to the bedroom. Then, he proceeded to show her how hungry he was for her.

By the time they were done, the toast was cold and inedible.

"Why don't we go to the main house and make a proper brunch?" he said with his hand on the small of her back. She had traded her sweatpants for a green skater dress after a quick shower.

"Your mum is probably downstairs by now. No way."

"If she's out of her room, then she's in the garden. You know how she feels about being in the house all day. By the time she comes in for lunch, we'll be done."

"Fine, but you have to go out first. I'll follow you in a few minutes."

"That's okay. I need to shower and change anyway. This is truly a walk of shame," he said with a laugh.

Before he left, she leaned in to steal one last kiss.

WHEN MAKENA WALKED into the main house half an hour later, David was already in the kitchen. He had changed into grey slacks and a black polo shirt and was in the process of dicing tomatoes. She joined him.

"Can I help?" she asked with a smile.

"No. Just sit there and keep me entertained. I'm making omelette and chips."

He had already done most of the work. The chips were already cooking, and he was almost done preparing ingredients for the omelette.

She sat on the high chair next to the countertops. It felt good to have someone do all the work for once. Unfortunately, it meant she couldn't keep her hands busy, and she was lost for what to do. She didn't know what to talk about with David. It was a strange feeling to have after they'd spent the night together. She also didn't want him to pry too much into her life.

"Gerald looks a lot like Charlie," he said.

She liked talking about her son, so he was a safe topic.

"He does. When he was born, he looked exactly like Charlie's baby photos. Thankfully, he is also just as smart as his uncle. His performance in school is impeccable," she said proudly.

"Yeah, Charlie is a genius. Did you know he graduated top of our class and got a fully paid scholarship for his MBA?"

Makena was surprised. She didn't even know Charlie got his MBA. He must have been at it around the time their parents died. They hadn't mentioned it, either, which meant he probably hadn't told them. He was so secretive with his life. But this was a good thing—they would all have been so proud of him.

"He never told us. When he graduated, he said that he had gotten a job and wouldn't be coming home. Our parents tried to persuade him to come home for a short while. They were so proud of him, they wanted to throw him a party. He said that he had already started the new job. They died never knowing how much more he had achieved," she said sadly. "What was he like in school?"

"He was quiet, always buried in his books. I was his only friend for years. We roomed together for a while. He hated living on campus, and I hated living with people who didn't know what ugali is," David said with a laugh.

He was almost done cooking, so she set the table. He brought the food and some Delmonte tropical juice. He served them both and sat opposite her.

"*Bon appetit*," he said.

"Thank you, this looks lovely," she said before getting started.

For a while, they ate in silence.

"What was school abroad like for you?" she asked.

"It was great. I was spoilt and overindulged. I enjoyed the full campus experience. That is until my father died just after my MBA graduation."

"I'm so sorry. That must have been hard. Why didn't you come back then?" she asked, curious. She knew how close he was with his mum; she would have assumed he would've returned to comfort her.

"I was back for a month, for the burial and to help get affairs in order. But we decided that I shouldn't give up on my dreams. Dad had put measures to ensure that Dukamart would continue even if neither Allison nor I were at the helm. I come back for AGMs, and I'm reachable on phone and email. The shares he left us meant that I was able to do what I wanted without worrying about my family," he answered, speaking of Dukamart, his family's chain of supermarkets.

Recently, they'd expanded and opened branches in Kampala, Dar es Salaam, and Kigali. The expansion had dominated business news for weeks because the supermarket business wasn't doing well in Kenya. Dukamart was a pleasant anomaly.

"That's nice," she said.

But it wasn't nice at all—she was thinking of how much money he and his family were worth. He must've noticed her frown because he perused her face for a long time.

"What do you do on your day off?" he asked, changing the conversation.

"I take Gerald somewhere fun. Sometimes, we go with Julia."

This Sunday was the only one she hadn't been with her son ever. When she said there was no leave of absence from parenting, she meant it. Aside from her stay at the hospital, she had never been away from her son for more than the school day. He didn't go for sleepovers or anywhere requiring him to be away overnight. She couldn't imagine getting a good night's sleep otherwise. And yet last night, wild horses wouldn't have woken her.

"Maybe I can take you two somewhere next Sunday," David said.

Makena stopped eating suddenly. She didn't know how to respond. He hadn't exactly asked her out on a date, which meant she had no reason to refuse outright. Sleeping together had changed the dynamics of their friendship, so she couldn't just presume he'd asked just for the sake of it.

"David, I... We can't. Nothing has changed. I still can't date, and we shouldn't involve Gerald. He can't think there's a chance of us being something we're not."

He reached across the table and held her hand. She felt her whole body shiver in response to the contact. Even with her mind in turmoil, her body recognised the touch of the man who had reawakened it.

"We're friends, that hasn't changed. Granted, I want us to be the kind of friends that have an occasional romp, but it doesn't mean I can't do something for you. This isn't a date. I just think Gerald could enjoy Go Karting. It's one of my favourite pastimes. You'll like it, too."

She had half a mind to object, but if she did, she would be depriving her son and herself of what seemed like a fun activity. Besides, she believed David was doing this out of the goodness of his heart and not to get her. He genuinely liked Gerald, so that helped.

"Okay, we can go."

Chapter Six

As Makena and Gerald had supper, he gushed over how much fun he'd had at Allison's. Before she brought him home, she'd taken the kids for pizza. Julia now had competition over who was Gerald's favourite aunt. She wasn't going to be happy about it, Makena thought as she got her son ready for bed. He was tired from the weekend's excitement, so there was no fight over his bedtime. He was out by eight p.m. She stayed up for a while to catch the show she was following.

Her cell phone beeped, and she checked—it was a text from David. She didn't even know she had his number.

David: Hello gorgeous,

I sneaked in my number this morning, hope you don't mind.

- D

She let out a laugh. Of course, he was the kind of person to sign off text messages with their initial. Very business-like.

Me: Hello,

I don't mind.

I wondered how u got it.

-M

She smiled at the fact he wouldn't even know she was making fun of him. Who even initializes their text in this country? He had been gone too long.

David: You should secure your phone.

-D

Me: He says after he has already taken advantage,

anyway, Gerald is the only one who takes it and I don't like being nagged

for the password every five minutes

-M

David: If you say so.

What are you wearing?

-D

This wasn't good. She was terrible at this, as in she had zero experience in flirting over text. She put the phone down and started thinking about how to get out of the conversation. It beeped again.

David: Kidding,

What are you doing?

-D

Me: Watching Muchaha Italiana on Citizen

-M

David: We're watching the same or rather, my mum is. I tuned out. But just so you know, her Italian accent is very un-convincing.

-D

Me: Hey, don't attack our show. Besides, how would you know how a convincing Italian accent sounds like?

-M

David: I just know.

Want a little morning romp tomorrow?

-D

Me: Much as I would love to, No time, kid and work.

-M

David: Skip yoga, I'll skip my run.

Leave your door unlocked when you take G to school.

-D

She didn't give him a definitive answer. They chatted a little more about her affinity for Mexican telenovelas and the fact he found them boring and dragged on. She missed most of *Muchacha Italiana,* and by the time she went to sleep, she was grinning ear to ear. She also knew she would be leaving the door open as he had asked.

MONDAY MORNINGS WERE usually rushed, with missing socks and incomplete homework. Gerald was a good kid, but he hated Mondays, the jump from weekend energy to school all day making him cranky. This Monday, however, it was like the universe was conspiring on Makena's behalf. So she embraced this new sense of positivity, and before she walked Gerald to school, she closed the door but didn't lock it. She texted David and also told him to ensure no one saw him. He texted back a winky face emoji.

When she got home, she quickly got in. It was dark with the curtains pulled, but the bedroom light was on, the sitting room empty. David was lounging on the bed nude, with a sheet across his waist. She bit her lip at the sight, her body growing hot in anticipation.

"Take off your clothes," he ordered, looking into her eyes.

She took off everything slowly, enjoying his heated gaze. It made her feel confident. She joined him in bed, naked, where he pulled her into a passionate kiss.

This time, their coupling was fast, and it had nothing to do with the time constraint. They both wanted each other desperately. Knowing how it was between them, it was hard not to.

They lay in each other's arms later, with his hands pulling her close and hers running through his chest hairs, twirling with the small curls.

His fingers lightly traced the scar on her arm, and she tensed.

"What happened here?" he asked.

"Clumsy youth," she answered quickly and took her hand away, closing the door on any further discussion. After several minutes, she spoke up. "We should probably come up with some ground rules."

"Wow, rules. Okay, let's hear them."

Makena pulled herself from his arms.

"David, we agreed that this isn't more than sex. We should have set some boundaries. Preferably before we slept with each other twice, but we should do that now."

She looked at him to gauge his reaction. He gave nothing away.

"I agree."

He pulled her back to him. She was tense and wouldn't relax her shoulders even to his touch.

"First off, we should keep this private, especially to our families. Charlie, who thinks I'm a mess, and your mother and sister, who are my bosses, shouldn't know that we're sleeping together. Also, this doesn't affect our friendship in any way, not in how you deal with Gerald or how we interact out of the bedroom. And finally, should either of us not want to do this anymore, we should be grown up enough to say it, not just be silent and ignore the other."

"That's all reasonable. I mean, my mother already warned me to stay away from you, I wouldn't want to incur her wrath."

He brought her hand back to his chest.

"I'm surprised by that. I didn't think your mum would be the type to warn her son against cavorting with the help." The offence in her voice was hard to hide, although she didn't even try.

"Don't be angry. It was actually for your benefit. She doesn't want me breaking your heart and then you'd leave, and she considers herself one of your people. I couldn't stop looking at you during Gianna's birthday, and she noticed."

"That's not going to happen," she said quickly. Before he could say anything, she extricated herself from him. "I need to get ready for work."

She grabbed a towel and went to the bathroom. The apartment didn't have a hot shower installed so she settled for a cold one. By the time she walked out of the bathroom, she was shaking from the cold, and David was gone. But she checked her phone, and he had sent her a text.

David: I'll be out for the day.

See you later.

-D

The text ended with a smiley face emoji. She smiled at the thoughtfulness. She sent him a reply wishing him a lovely day and went about getting ready for work.

THE WEEK FLEW BY, AND David and Makena managed to sneak in another tryst, just as passionate. They texted at least once a day. She found herself looking forward to hearing from him. She enjoyed talking to him about her day. She had only one friend, Julia, and it was good to have another.

She wondered what he did now. He left every morning, sometimes in a suit, and came home in the evening like a regular guy with a nine-to-five, but he hadn't mentioned getting a job to her. She didn't want to pry, so she just kept her thoughts to herself. She also wondered whether he was still up for taking them Go Karting. He hadn't brought it up again, and she hadn't told Gerald because she didn't want to get his hopes up.

On Saturday evening, as she watched a movie with Gerald, her phone rang—David. She was surprised because he never called. She went to the bedroom.

"Hello," she said almost in a whisper.

"Hello, gorgeous. How are you?"

"I'm good. What's up?"

"Nothing much. I had quite a day and wanted to hear your voice. It's lovely, even when you're whispering. Why are you whispering?"

She let out a laugh.

"I don't know. It just happened," she replied, not whispering.

He laughed. "Never mind that. I wanted to remind you about Go Karting tomorrow."

"We're still going?" She hadn't made other plans, but she hadn't held out hope he would go through with it. This was why she hadn't told Gerald.

"I said we would, didn't I?" David sighed, then he added, "One thing I want you to know about, Makena, is that I will always keep my word. In the small things or big things, I don't make promises I can't keep."

She was silent for a while. That was a heavy implication, and she didn't know what to do with it. She didn't understand why he felt the need to make it.

"Okay," she said.

"What are you doing tonight?"

She told him about the movie they were watching. He was on his way to meet friends for drinks. He told her to be ready at nine the next morning. They were going to Whistling Moran in Athi River, about an hour's drive from his house.

AT NINE THE NEXT MORNING, David knocked on Makena's door. She and Gerald were ready. He asked Gerald to bring his skates, which added to the excitement. They got into his car, and he drove off. Gerald was a little mad he wasn't allowed to ride in the front seat, but they made it up to him by letting him play with David's phone. He said it had cooler games than hers.

"How was your week?" David asked Makena.

"It was great. It was off to a great start and kept getting better," she said about their Monday morning hookup.

He laughed. "You're welcome."

"What about you? What have you been up to?"

"I've had a few business meetings throughout the week. I'm still thinking about how long I should stay and what that would mean. The longest I've stayed here since my dad died was a month. It's already been longer than that now, and I need a plan for what comes next."

"How come you've stayed so long this time?"

She hoped it wasn't for her sake. He'd told her he liked her before, and she realised they'd spent a lot of time together. Although she liked him, too, and relished the time they spent together, the last thing she would want was for him to upend his life for her sake. She didn't even know how long it would be before Paul found them, and then, they'd have to leave. She'd been through the drill several times before, but she'd never had to leave someone behind. She didn't want to have this kind of responsibility.

"I've been concerned about my mum's health. Right before we hired you, she had been hospitalised for a week. She'll never admit it, but she hasn't been okay in a long time. I want to be here long enough to gauge her myself. Also, I was homesick."

She struggled to imagine him as being homesick. He had an air of confidence and self-awareness around him which made it hard to imagine him being held back by something as trivial as homesickness.

They drove in silence for a while, and then he asked,

"Who else have you worked for aside from my overbearing mother?"

She thought about it for a while.

"At this point, I think I've done everything. My most memorable job was as a waitress. It was early on when Gerald was much younger. I don't even like to remember the things I saw, and yet, I can't seem to forget." She shuddered jokingly at the memory. "I was a barista at a coffee shop when I was on campus. Trust me, if you haven't sold a piping hot pumpkin spice latte to a sorority girl who then dumps it in the trash for being burnt and throws toddler-like tantrums, then you haven't lived. I have a lot of respect for people in the service industry." She glanced his way. "What are you doing now? While you wait to decide on what next."

"I applied for a job at Dukamart HQ. They need a head of accounting. If I decide to stay, this will put me on the track for CFO on merit rather than taking the obvious route of nepotism."

They both laughed. He would get the job. Somehow, Makena knew it wasn't all nepotism. Based on what she had learnt from his mother and her brother, he had a very impressive CV.

They had a fun-filled day where they all got to race on go-karts, and Gerald skated to his heart's content without restrictions. On their way home, Makena insisted on buying them all KFC. She was hellbent on paying for it herself since David had paid much more at Whistling Moran. By the time they got home a little after seven p.m., Gerald was out like a light. David wanted to carry him in, but she woke him up to change and brush his teeth. When he was all tucked in, she joined David on the couch.

"Thank you. We had a lot of fun today," she whispered so as not to wake Gerald.

"I did, too. You and Gerald sure know how to throw down. Check your WhatsApp, I sent you something,"

She grabbed her phone from the table and opened her messages. There was a photo from David, of her and Gerald bumping into each other on the go-karts in the red overalls and white helmet they were given for safety. They were both laughing out loud, her head thrown back in joy.

"The only other time I have seen that look of pure joy on your face was when you were on the trampoline," David said.

Makena smiled.

"That's because he has me acting like a kid. I forget the scam that is being an adult when I'm with him."

She got up to make them some tea. He pulled her to him, saying he didn't want any. She lay her head on her shoulder, still as a rod.

"Relax," he said, squeezing her shoulder.

She raised her head to look at him.

"What gives you pure joy?" she asked him.

"I could tell you, or I could show you." He moved to kiss her neck, and she pulled back. He pulled away from her, too. "I know, I know. Sorry, I lost myself for a moment. I think I'll have that tea now."

Makena busied herself with preparing tea, trying not to knock any dishes around. She could hear Gerald's soft snore and didn't want to wake him. David turned on the TV and lowered the volume—it was time for *Muchacha Italiana*, and he laughed at the sight.

"If you're going to laugh rather than sit silently and watch, you better leave," she said jokingly as she set the tea and sat next to him on the couch. He took a sip. It seemed he liked his tea hot and without sugar because he sighed in contentment. She added two teaspoons of sugar to hers and lifted it, and just before she took a sip, she blew at it to lower the temperature. He tensed next to her, and she marvelled at the effect she had on him over such a mundane gesture.

"Slow your roll, mister," she said with a laugh.

"It's not my fault that everything you do is a major turn-on. Come on, watch your soap opera, and I will work on some of those knots on your shoulders. You're always so tense, I worry you'll break."

He massaged her shoulders through her clothing, which did nothing to protect her from the heat of his touch. She let out a sigh which progressed into a moan as she leaned into his touch. Then she yawned, proving she was more tired than turned on.

They both chuckled, her in embarrassment and him in amusement. He kept massaging her and felt her completely relax in his arms. She struggled to keep her eyes open because it felt so good and she wanted to savour the feeling, but in the end, the excitement of the day caught up with her just like it had her son.

Chapter Seven

Makena woke up feeling blissfully relaxed. Her alarm hadn't even rung yet. She checked the time on her phone, and it was fifteen minutes before she had to be up. She didn't even remember coming to bed. There was a text from David telling her he had left the previous night and he had an early morning meeting at Dukamart HQ so wish him luck.

"Good luck, David," she whispered.

She sent him a text thanking him for the day before and wishing him a lovely day. She didn't think he needed it, but he had asked. Since she'd woken up early, she had time to make Gerald his favourite breakfast of fluffy pancakes.

He was thrilled and didn't even fight her when she hugged him at the school gate. She turned around to walk home, thrilled at how her morning was going.

Ricky stepped beside her and started walking alongside. He didn't give her the chance to use her earphones to ignore him.

"It's been a while, Mama Gerald. How have you been?"

Makena decided to bypass open hostility and try to shake him off politely.

"I have been well, and busy with work," she answered. "I have to get going now. I need to start work."

"Great, we're headed in the same direction. I'm going to pick up my Range Rover from the garage."

She realised this wasn't going to be an easy shake-off. She started walking faster to make the short walk over and done as fast as possible.

"I see you have started dating. I've seen your boyfriend bringing Gerald to school a few times, and my son says Gerald can't stop talking about him."

She tensed. This was exactly what she had wanted to avoid, the speculation over her non-existent relationship with David.

"David is a friend. He walks Gerald to school when he's doing his morning run."

Ricky chuckled.

"In that case, you're still available. Mama Gerald, you have no idea the things I could do for you. I could open a business for you so you don't have to slave for someone else every day. I could rent you a nice-looking apartment, hell, maybe even buy you a house. Being a single mother is hard. I will make your life easier. All you have to do is say yes to me. Become my—"

She cut him off, unable to hear any more of that drivel.

"Become your what? Not your wife because you already have one of those. Girlfriend? Again, you're married, so you can't have a girlfriend. Mistress? No, thank you. I respect myself too much for that, and most importantly, as I have said a hundred times, I'm not interested."

He looked taken aback by her stern rebuttal, but he quickly recovered and gave her a menacing look.

"Everyone has a price, baby. I will figure you out one of these days. You pretend to be this saint, but so long as you're dragging around that boy of yours without a father, you're just another whore. The least you can do is own up to it."

Makena walked off, but she didn't take his words lightly. She felt his gaze follow her as she walked to the gate, opened it, and stepped in without looking back. She waited until she was in her house then leaned against the door and sighed heavily.

All the joy of that morning was gone. Being shamed for being a single mother was nothing new, so it barely registered. It was the other part she was concerned about. She could still feel his stare as he said he would figure her out. The last thing she wanted was for anyone to try and figure her out. While she kept her tracks well hidden, she wasn't exactly in witness protection, and with enough money and interest, figuring her out could happen just like that. Then everything she had built would be gone just as quickly, and she would have to start over.

THAT NIGHT, SHE HAD the same nightmare she'd been having since she'd left Paul. She had just had a baby—the face would alternate depending on the night. This time, it was Gerald. She was exhausted but stretched out her arms to receive the baby from the nurse. The nurse looked from her to the baby, then asked, "Why did you do this to your baby?" She put the bundle in her arms. Makena looked down. The baby had been beaten bloody. She looked around—she was in the bedroom of her old house. Paul was looking at her, smirking, fidgeting with his gun. Then, he aimed it at the baby in her arms, and without a single emotion passing over his face, he pulled the trigger. Makena screamed, before waking up to her son gently shaking her and calling out to her.

"Are you okay?" he asked.

She pulled him into a hug and nodded.

"I'm fine. I'm sorry I woke you."

Gerald didn't say anything. It wasn't the first time he'd been the one to pull her out of a nightmare. She felt terrible that he was put in such a position. It was two a.m. She got out of bed and turned the light in the sitting room on so he could go back to bed behind the partition delineating his space in the single bedroom they shared. She poured herself a glass of water because she suddenly felt parched, then downed it and got back into bed.

After what she thought couldn't have been more than ten minutes, the shrill ring of her alarm woke her up. She reached blindly for her phone and pulled it from under her pillow. The light from the screen was blinding. She quickly hit the snooze button and gave in to the wave of darkness that overcame her, only to be pulled out of it by the alarm five minutes later. She checked the time and realised she was cutting it close. She needed to get up and get Gerald ready for school.

Her head could barely lift from the pillow, it weighed a ton, and she felt hot and clammy. She had sweated through her clothes. Her stomach roiled, and her head was throbbing. Still, she dragged herself out of bed.

She'd barely made it to the door when she felt the darkness overtake her. She heard the bedroom door open, but try as she might, she couldn't muster the energy to open her eyes. She slipped back to darkness again. She heard voices, and then felt someone lift her and carry her—she felt the cold air hit her and knew she must be outside. She slipped out of consciousness again.

The next time she woke up, she was able to open her eyes and look around. She was in David's car in the back seat, strapped in, her head resting comfortably on a pillow. He was driving.

"David, where are we going?" she asked softly.

He looked at her through the rearview mirror. She was overwhelmed by the concern in his eyes.

"We're going to the hospital."

"No, wait, turn around. I have to go make breakfast for Gerald and get him ready for school." She tried to sit up, but her entire body was in pain.

"It's taken care of, don't worry. The breakfast part, that is. The maid will make sure he's fed. He won't be going to school today, though. He was terrified when he called me. I don't think he'll be okay until he knows you're fine. Which is why you should cooperate and let me get you checked out. The hospital isn't far, and the doctor is already waiting. I called ahead."

"Gerald called you?"

She felt even worse—he'd had to wake her out of the nightmare and then find her unconscious on the floor. From the time Gerald knew how to handle a phone, she'd made sure he knew to call Julia in case of an emergency. He had Makena's number memorised, however many times she changed it. She was impressed at the forethought he'd had to call David instead. David was better placed to help.

She was still in her pyjamas which were drenched in sweat. She was embarrassed but glad David had been there to help. She knew he'd had to fight with Gerald to convince him she would be okay so he agreed to be left at home.

"He was a little scared and wanted to come. But we came to an agreement. I promised him you'd be okay and you'd call him as soon as the doctor saw you, and he promised to eat his breakfast and not give the maid a hard time. He's a good boy. Your phone is on the seat next to you if you want to talk to him. My mum will put him through."

He pulled up in the parking lot of the small private hospital where she sometimes brought his mother for her checkups.

David helped her out of the car and into the hospital. She couldn't even stand on her own, and she felt as if a rock band were playing in her head. She walked tentatively even though he held her hand. She didn't trust that she wouldn't fall again. He sat her in the waiting area and went to talk to the reception-ist. A minute later, the doctor showed up. Makena had met him before—he was Mrs. Mutua's doctor.

"How are you feeling, Makena?" he asked.

"Terrible, like death warmed over."

The doctor motioned for a wheelchair to be brought, and she was wheeled to an examination room, leaving David in the waiting area. She told the doctor her symptoms, and he exam-ined her. A nurse came in and did a blood draw. A wave of nausea hit her, and she threw up everything she had eaten or drunk.

The doctor asked the nurse to bring her a hospital gown to change into and put her on an IV drip. He allowed David to come and sit with her while she waited for her test results.

"Don't you have to go to work? Now that you're gainfully employed?" she asked with a weak laugh.

He was dressed in a shirt and jeans and still had his morn-ing stubble. He had texted her the previous night to let her know he would be starting work today.

"When I took the job, I didn't know the dramatic lengths you would go to to make me spend my mornings with you.

Otherwise, I would have considered staying home like the trust fund baby that I am."

She smiled and reached out for his hand, and he gave it to her.

"Thank you," she said, her voice heavy with emotion. She hoped he would chalk it up to whatever was ailing her.

Before he could respond, the doctor came in and asked him to leave.

"Makena, it seems you have contracted typhoid."

She was surprised at the unexpected diagnosis.

"Don't worry, it's nothing two days in the hospital and a course of antibiotics can't treat."

Her heart skipped a beat, and her hand flew to her chest. She shook her head. The last time she'd been admitted to the hospital, she'd been recovering from the beating Paul had inflicted on her. She hadn't seen her son in weeks. She couldn't do this to him again.

"No, Doctor. I have a son, and he doesn't have anyone else. I'll just take the meds home."

"If you want to be well enough to take care of him, you have to take care of yourself. Otherwise, you will be back here soon, and it could be much worse."

She wondered what could be worse than collapsing next to your bed first thing in the morning.

"Look, just to reassure you, your son can visit for thirty minutes every day that you're here. Which, if you follow the course of treatment, won't be more than two days."

"Fine," she said reluctantly.

She was put in a wheelchair and taken to the small ward. When she was assigned a private room, she tried to resist because she knew there was no way NHIF would cover this, but the doctor was adamant. He said the room wasn't in use anyway.

Once she was settled, David came in to say goodbye. He'd brought her her phone.

"Goodbye. Have fun in the outside world of the healthy," she said, her voice dripping with mirth.

"Don't be grumpy. You'll be home soon enough. I'll bring Gerald in the evening. Text me everything you need, and I'll bring it, too."

He kissed her forehead and left.

She grabbed her phone and called David's mum, who reassured her that taking care of Gerald for a few days wouldn't be a bother and refused to hear of Julia picking him up. Makena was conflicted about calling Julia anyway as she was heavily pregnant. She spoke to Gerald and let him know she had been admitted. She could tell he was taken aback by the news, but he was brave about it. He was relieved to hear he was allowed to visit her and couldn't wait. She called Julia, too, but insisted she not visit her. She wouldn't be staying long anyway. She also called Gerald's school to let them know he wouldn't be coming to school.

Less than an hour later, she was done and left with nothing to do but wait to see if the medication worked. Her drip had been switched for one which contained her dosage. There was a TV in the room and magazines on the bedside table. The nurse had given her the Wi-Fi password. The TV even had Netflix. She surfed for a bit then decided to watch *Modern Family* for the umpteenth time—she found the comedy always lifted her spirit.

She must have dozed off because the next time she awoke, it was lunchtime. The food was nice, for hospital food, but she had just a few bites before her stomach roiled and she pushed the plate aside. The nurse changed her IV drip which was already empty. She was feeling much better. Her fever was still there, and she had a headache and stomachache, but the dizziness was gone.

In the evening, David came with Gerald, as promised. He also brought her several things she had asked for, including underwear as she had left the house with only the clothes on her back. Gerald was happy to see her conscious and speaking, but he still expressed concern over the IV drip. They assured him it was the best way to ensure the medicine worked fast. Makena asked David whether he would mind taking him to school the next day since she didn't want him missing too much. After a while, they said goodbye and left.

A two-day stay at the hospital wasn't as long or gruelling as she'd thought it would be. Soon, she was back home with a five-day prescription of antibiotics and a warning to stay off any heavy lifting for at least a week. It earned her a week off from work. Although David offered to bring her meals and walk Gerald to school, she refused to take his help. She was well enough to cook and walk ten minutes. The laundry piled up, but she would get to it when she was back to full gear.

She spent the week working on something she had been thinking about for months. When she went to college, the plan had always been to finish her diploma and enrol for a degree immediately after. It was something she had discussed with her parents because she wanted a solid career in social work. They had promised to pay for her education until she was done.

Their death had derailed that. Charlie had paid for her diploma, but by the time she was done, she'd been pregnant with Gerald, and plans of furthering her education or getting a job had been shelved.

She'd been thinking about enrolling for a degree. She wasn't in a solid place yet and constantly worried about having to run if Paul found them. However, a lot of universities were offering online classes, so she could study from anywhere.

She researched the best course combination and the university which would offer her the best options. Although she didn't have the financial aspect figured out, she liked having the information in handy. She also didn't like the idea of being idle for an entire week. She sent out emails requesting course content and fee structures.

Chapter Eight

Makena's new quest provided a refreshing change of pace. After seeing Gerald off to school and making breakfast for her boss, she set about doing the week's laundry. She took a break for lunch before getting back to it. It was late afternoon by the time all of it had been hung to dry.

Although she and David had been texting, they hadn't seen each other in person since he'd dropped her off at home from the hospital. He had been extremely busy at work, and she was preoccupied with her plans, son, and work. She also still felt disconcerted by how much she had come to rely on him. Although she missed him, she appreciated the distance. She hadn't been quite this dependent on anyone in years, and she didn't want to get used to it. Over the weekend, Julia had come visiting, and she had enjoyed her company. She hadn't told her what was going on between her and David because she didn't want to make it a bigger deal than it was.

On Sunday, she had taken Gerald swimming in a nearby hotel. He'd learnt to swim in one of the schools she had taken him to, and although nothing beat skating in his list of fun activities, he enjoyed doing it once in a while. She was also finalizing plans for Julia's baby shower which was set for the following Sunday. She had booked the venue at a picturesque hotel just outside the city. She enlisted Julia's husband Henry for the surprise—he had to make sure she wasn't occupied for the day.

She had heard back from most of the schools she'd emailed and had a tentative idea about where she would be going for her degree. She would have to wait until the following year to apply, but this just gave her more time to plan for it.

On Saturday, she went with Julia's friend to town to shop for the baby shower. She picked her up just after breakfast, and she'd left Gerald watching TV. He knew not to leave the compound, so she knew he would be safe. She came back just in time for lunch. The friend took the baby shower things as she was in charge of getting the venue ready while Makena made sure Julia showed up.

She found Gerald skating on the driveway and David on one of the benches on the grass. She waved at him, and he stood to join her before she opened the door. She had a shopping bag with some clothes she'd bought for Gerald and her white dress for the baby shower. She stopped to wait for him.

"Hi," she greeted.

He stopped in front of her. "Good to see you back on your feet. You've been busy."

They shook hands and lingered for a moment longer. She was startled by the heat from his warm hand. She smiled at him and pulled hers back.

"As have you. How is work?"

She placed her bags by the door and walked towards the bench he had just vacated. She didn't want them talking just outside her door, as that was bound to attract attention. He joined her.

"It's fast-paced. I haven't been this busy since I was a student. Most days, I get home late at night. The new branches we opened in Uganda and Rwanda are doing well. There are talks of even more expansion. I like being back at work. I was climbing walls having nothing to do."

"I can just imagine. I'm glad you're liking it. Do they call you Mr. Mutua? Because that, I would love to see," she asked with a laugh.

"Of course, I'm the boss. Well, for the accounting department, at least. I joined the company amid the quarterly reports. That's why I've been so busy. It was terrible of the previous guy to leave in the midst of it all. I had to get caught up and then take it from where he left off."

As Makena listened to him, she marvelled at how passionately he talked about his job. It wasn't just his father's corporation—it was a place where he was doing the work he loved.

"Is it different from what you used to do in the States?" she asked.

"It's different. For one, I wasn't head of accounting. I worked for an auditing firm. It wasn't as fast-paced as it is here. Even before I came, I knew I was done there. There was no opportunity for growth for me. I tried to get a promotion for years, but I kept being passed over. Eventually, I decided I was done. My boss tried to convince me to stay, promising me that I would be promoted the next time. I had made my decision already, though."

"Well, people do tend to not value what they have until they lose it. It seems the decision worked well for you."

"Yeah, they do," he said. "Gerald tells me you have plans for tomorrow, your friend Julia's baby shower."

"Yeah, I just came from shopping for it with a friend of hers."

"Will you be taking Gerald? I ask because I don't think he will have a lot of fun being the only kid in a whole group of grownups."

"He's used to it. I take him everywhere. I'll be gone all day, and I can't leave him alone."

"You don't have to. You can leave him with me. We're taking Nathan and Gianna bike riding, and he can come with us."

Makena was reluctant. She didn't want to impose on family time.

"I'd prefer it if he came with me. I don't want to impose, plus he doesn't know how to ride a bike."

"I'll teach him, and Nathan and Gianna love him. They'll be thrilled for him to be there," David said.

Eventually, she complied, conceding that Gerald would have more fun with his fellow kids than with her and a bunch of ladies at a baby shower.

She went inside to make lunch. Later in the evening, she called Julia and told her to pick her up tomorrow. She just told her she wanted to go out with her and didn't give too much detail.

AFTER BREAKFAST THE next morning, she checked Gerald's homework to ensure he had none left. She wouldn't be home until late in the evening, and he had a habit of ambushing her with incomplete homework on Mondays. He still had a bit to do, and she got him to do it by threatening to stop him from going biking.

By midday, they were both ready. She put on light makeup and wore her white dress and black heels. Julia came to pick her up, and she took Gerald to the main house to wait until it was time to leave. David promised to have him home in one piece and call her if anything happened.

The drive to the hotel where the baby shower was held was half an hour. People had already texted on the group chat that they had arrived and were putting up the decorations. Makena texted them to let them know they were on their way.

"Nice of you to dress up for me," Julia said with a laugh.

"I'm a single mother with no social life. Any chance I get to dress up, I do it," she said, diverting Julia's attention.

"Okay, whatever you say. I don't get why we didn't just go to Garden City, though." Her house was in Garden Estate which was close to Garden City.

"I'm sorry. I didn't think about how long the drive would be. I just thought we could do something different today. We used to go to this hotel for the music back then."

Julia was eight months pregnant, and having her drive around was thoughtless on her part. Although she hadn't said it, Makena could see she was having a hard time. She texted Henry to come and get them when the baby shower was done, and he agreed.

"Don't worry about it, I could use a fun afternoon," Julia said.

"How are you feeling?"

"I'm alternating between sheer terror at the thought of pushing a whole human from my body and looking forward to meeting my baby. I'm also concerned she will end up with a horrible name. We still haven't settled on one. My husband insists on vetoing all of my choices, and his are nothing I want on my child's birth certificate."

Makena laughed. These were all common worries of a soon-to-be mum. She could still remember Paul's suggestions for baby names. Each left her more horrified than the next. They decided on Gerald hours after he was already born. The name hadn't even been on their lists of suggestions.

"It's normal to feel like that. Just don't let yourself worry too much. You're much more prepared than I was. That nursery is gorgeous," Makena said. Julia had sent her photos of her baby's nursery which they had decorated over the past week.

"You were young when you had Gerald, and you're a great mum," Julia said as she pulled up at the hotel. She parked the car and turned to her. "This is a wonderful place for my baby shower, thank you."

Makena was so surprised, she looked at her questioningly.

"Henry can't keep a secret. I've known all week. I'm stealing that look on your face when they yell surprise," Julia said laughing.

She pulled Makena in a hug, and then they got out of the car.

HENRY AND JULIA DROPPED her off at eight p.m. They'd had so much fun, played games and showering Julia and her unborn baby with gifts and love. Makena was thrilled to have planned it. Julia's surprise face was so good, the girls hadn't found her out.

David had texted her earlier to let her know they were back home and they'd had fun. She had barely thought about Gerald all day. It was a sign she trusted David with him, which surprised her.

She rang the bell in the main house, and the maid opened. David and Gerald were on the couch watching a movie. They had succeeded in taking over the TV from David's mother. She sat on the other side looking bored by whatever they were watching.

"Did you have fun?" she asked her son.

"Yeah, we did. I learnt how to ride a bike, then Uncle David let go, and I didn't fall," Gerald said excitedly.

"Wow, that's great. Maybe now, you can teach me," she said.

"Uncle David will teach you. He's much better at it. You can use my bike."

Makena thought she'd misunderstood because Gerald didn't have a bike.

"You don't have a bike," she said.

"I do. Uncle David bought me one."

She turned abruptly to face David, lost for words. He must have missed the look of horror on her face.

"No need to thank me. Nathan and Gianna have them, and I didn't want him to feel left out," he said.

Makena stood up abruptly.

"Thank you?" she asked, then shook her head. She took Gerald's hand. "We have to go home. Have a lovely night."

As she opened the door, she heard Mrs. Mutua tell David, "I told you."

Gerald was disappointed about being pulled away from his movie, but Makena didn't leave room for debate. She quickly had him brush his teeth and get into bed then sat down on the couch. She pulled her phone out. There was a text from David apologizing. She thought about it for a minute then called him. It rang a few times, then he picked up.

"I'm sorry," he said. "I shouldn't have bought him a bike without asking first. I didn't plan on it, but he was looking at it so longingly."

"I knew he wanted one, but I was going to buy him one for his birthday. I just don't like him thinking he can get things just because he wants them. I don't want him to be a brat."

"Gerald is a good kid. He won't turn into a brat just because he got a bike. But I'm still sorry I bought it without telling you. My mum told me it was a bad idea as soon as she saw it."

"She's wise," Makena said. "Obviously, I will refund you whatever you spent on the bike. I was saving up for one, anyway."

David knew better than to argue. She asked him to let her know how much it had cost.

"He rode so well, I felt compelled to buy it. He's a quick study and didn't fall once."

"He is, although that's an improvement from when he was learning to skate. He fell so many times that I was one step from setting the skates on fire. He even broke his hand once. It was horrifying." She shuddered at the memory.

"He's a kid. They like risking themselves for adventure. They know someone will take care of them regardless."

"You have no idea. Raising a boy as a single mum is an extreme sport. You never know what they'll break next or what dangerous hobby they'll pick up next. Gerald went through a jumping phase as a toddler. He would climb on things and jump. The bigger he got, the higher the jump. His father once caught him trying to get on top of the cupboard. My heart stopped for a minute."

It was only when she was done recounting the memory that she realized how, for the first time, she had willingly mentioned Gerald's father to David.

He was silent for a minute then he spoke.

"According to my mum, I was much worse."

His words skipped over the awkwardness.

"I went house hunting last week," he said.

Makena took in a sharp intake of air. "You're moving out?"

She felt a lump in her throat and swallowed. She had gotten used to having him around— she didn't like how it made her feel bereft.

"Yeah, I need to be closer to work. It takes an hour or more most days to get to Mombasa Road. I need to be closer for the sake of my sanity. Sitting in traffic all that long is maddening."

"Have you found anything promising?"

"Yeah, I actually found an amazing three-bedroom. I will take a day off this week to shop for furnishings then move in over the weekend."

Makena stopped herself from asking what a single man needed a three-bedroom house for. It was none of her business.

"It sounds like you're putting down roots. A job, an apartment. Have you decided to stay for good, after all?"

"Not exactly. I'm still thinking about it. I just didn't want to be idle while I do it. Also, I miss my independence and freedom. There's only so much of it you can have, even in your mid-thirties, if you're living with your mother."

She laughed as she remembered the lengths they had to go to hide their trysts from his mother. They talked for a while and then said goodnight.

It had been almost two months since David had arrived in their lives. He'd had the worst opinion of her, and she had been determined not to let him in. Without meaning to, she hadn't just let him in but opened her heart wide for him. Just as he was planning his departure from their lives, Makena realized she had fallen in love with him.

Somewhere along the way, the feelings she had for him had developed into something whose depth she couldn't fathom. Which meant it was probably for the best that he was leaving. She had set the rules of their relationship, and she had broken the greatest one of them. She couldn't set herself up for the pain that could come from allowing this to continue.

Chapter Nine

After David moved out, their communication deteriorated to an occasional text. Makena missed him terribly, but she knew being with him wouldn't do her any good. When, not if, the time came to run after Paul found them, the heartbreak would be much worse.

She kept herself busy with work. She also started thinking about how she would pay her school fees. She had decided she wouldn't ask Charlie. However, it would take her years of saving before she could even afford a single semester. The remaining option was a loan. If she was lucky, she could get a HELB loan. She was worried her age would affect her eligibility, but it didn't hurt to try.

She was also helping Julia with some last-minute shopping for the baby. She had gotten her a stuffed toy fish for the nursery, which Julia loved.

Two weeks after the baby shower and about a week before her due date, Julia went into labour. Henry called Makena while they were on the way to the hospital. Since Julia was her go-to babysitter, she had to leave Gerald with Mrs. Mutua and her maid. It was on a weekend, so she didn't have to worry about school. By the time she got to the hospital, Julia was in active labour, and her baby girl was born a few hours later. After she was cleaned and Julia transferred to a private room, she was allowed to see them.

"She's adorable," Makena said as she held her, the baby bundled in a yellow blanket and asleep. "Have you found a name yet?"

"Yes, we're naming her Lily," Julia said. She looked tired, but she gazed at her daughter adoringly. Henry held her hand and kissed the back of it.

Makena loved the name. "A beautiful name for a beautiful baby."

After a while, she handed the baby back to Julia and went to get coffee.

As she sipped the hot coffee at the hospital cafeteria, a thought crossed her mind and filled her with terror. It could be because she had just met her best friend's baby. Whatever it was, it hit her she might be pregnant. It had been almost two months since she'd had her period. She tracked it through an app on her phone, just to keep up with her cycle. She hadn't had to worry about it in four years. She and David had used protection—they were both strict on that— but there had been one instance where things had gotten so hot and heavy, they had split.

Now with the thought in her head, she couldn't escape it. She could just imagine a baby that was half her, half David. It would be adorable.

But before she could allow the thought to blossom, she thought about her complicated life. How could she think about bringing another child into that? How could she allow it to happen? She shook her head violently, causing a passerby to stop and ask if she was okay.

She quickly stood up. Before she allowed herself to go into the rabbit hole of possibilities, she had to know for sure. She couldn't find out alone, not while she was this close to hyperventilating just from the thought of it. Her heart beat fast, and her hands shook as she dialled David's number.

There was loud music in the background. She almost chickened out, but it quieted down.

"I need to tell you something," she said after they'd greeted each other.

"Okay, I'm listening."

"It really needs to be in person. Let me know when you're not busy."

"How about today? You can come to my place."

She thought for a while, then she nodded. "Okay, let me know how to get there."

"Where are you? I'll order you an Uber."

She had half a mind to refuse, but she decided to accept it. It would be quicker and more convenient.

"I'm at Coptic Hospital. Julia had her baby today."

"That's great. Tell her congratulations on my behalf. Wait for my call about the cab."

She called Mrs. Mutua to ask if Gerald could sleep over, which she was okay with. Makena went and bought three pregnancy tests from the pharmacy. Then she said goodbye to Julia, Henry, and their baby. The cab arrived, and she got on it.

It took twenty minutes to get to Nairobi West where David lived. The neighbourhood was serene and cool with tall trees and sparse, sprawling apartments. The building he lived in had ten floors from her count. It was surrounded by a stone wall and had a brown metal gate.

He was waiting for her outside the gate. His gaze roamed over her body when she stepped out of the cab. As soon as he paid the cab driver, he pulled her into a hug.

"I missed you," he said.

Makena's heart swelled with warmth. She didn't know how much she'd needed to hear him say that.

"Me, too," she said.

He let her go and led her inside the gate. They got into the elevator and rode it to the ninth floor. He opened the door and led her inside.

The spacious living room was exactly what she thought his living space would be. The large windows were covered with velvet navy blue curtains, the same colour as his seven-seater velvet Chesterfield sofa set. She took off her shoes and stepped on the soft grey carpet. He pointed her to one of the seats, and she sank down and placed her bag next to her.

"Can I get you something to drink?" he asked.

She eyed the glass of wine he must have been drinking before she arrived on the glass coffee table. Then, she remembered that she might be pregnant and asked for a glass of water instead.

He joined her on the couch. "I'm glad you called, because I need to talk to you, too. I know it doesn't bode well for me that I waited until you called, and I'm sorry for that."

She decided to let him talk first. It would give her time to gather her thoughts.

"Okay, tell me."

He took her hand. Her nerves didn't prevent her from heating up at his touch.

"I like you," he said. "I know we said that we were just sleeping together, but it's more than that for me. I have missed you so much, and I want more. I want to take you on dates, take you on adventures. I want us to spend evenings together, relaxing over wine and a movie. I want for there to be the possibility of us having a future together."

He was saying everything she would have wanted to hear if she weren't so nervous. She wanted everything he said he wanted, but that wasn't what her life had in store for her. There was also the small matter of a possible pregnancy which could change everything.

In her experience, words weren't always backed up by action. Unfortunately, his words would be tested much sooner than he would have anticipated.

He leaned in to kiss her, and she gave herself in to the kiss. It was slow and sensual and filled her with heat. She wanted more than anything to get it on, right there on the couch.

He pulled away, and she kept her eyes closed for half a second longer, feeling bereft of his touch. She opened them, and their eyes locked. He waited for her to talk.

"David, I don't know how to tell you this."

He must be able tell she was nervous because she was no longer looking into his eyes.

He took her hand in his. "It's okay, Makena. You can tell me anything. I don't want you to feel rushed into anything. If you don't want this, we can take as much time as you want, until you're ready."

"It's not that, it's... I think I'm pregnant."

He was quiet for a long while.

"I haven't tested or anything," she continued. "But I suspect I am, from that one time. I haven't gotten my period since, and I hadn't thought about it until today when I saw Julia's baby. Anyway, I bought a bunch of tests. I just couldn't do it alone. That's why I called you."

She was speaking too fast, and then she opened her bag and started digging for the tests. When she couldn't find them fast enough, she spilt the entire contents on the coffee table, looking for them.

David grabbed her hands just as she was about to embark on the task of spreading everything around.

"Slow down," he said.

She looked at him in surprise, suspicious of his mellow reaction to all this. "You're not worried?"

"No. First of all, there is nothing to be mad, worried, panicked, or concerned about. Until there is, I think we should stay away from any of those feelings. Second, I want you to know that should there be something, we're in this together. It takes two, and it will be the two of us dealing with this. You're not alone."

He hugged her, and for the first time, Makena started to believe that it wasn't a disaster. When he released her, he grabbed the tests and gave them to her, then showed her to the bathroom.

When she emerged from the bathroom ten minutes later, all three tests in hand, relief filled her. She displayed the single line on the tests to him.

"Not pregnant. We dodged a bullet," she said and then threw herself into his embrace.

David held her tight. "For the record, I wouldn't consider you and I having a baby as a bullet."

She threw the tests into the trash and joined him on the couch, where she took the glass of wine and downed it in one gulp.

"You say that now," she said.

"I'm serious. When you're ready, we can talk about that happening for us. I have always wanted kids, and I'm sure Gerald would love having a sibling."

"I know he would, but not like this. Not when we just started talking about dating."

"I agree. We'll be careful so that if it happens, we'll be ready for it and happy about it."

His eyes suddenly seemed like he had been transported to a different time.

"Are you okay?" she asked with concern.

"Yeah, this just took me back..." He paused for a long moment. "A year ago, I had a conversation just like this with my ex-girlfriend, only that time, I didn't dodge a bullet. She was pregnant. I was okay with it, but she didn't want to have a baby. She was in the middle of an intensive master's program and was working. I tried to convince her that we could do this, but she didn't want to. I was heartbroken, but I went with her to the clinic and helped her out as she recovered. Soon after, we broke up. I understood what a difficult choice it was for her, but that didn't stop me from longing for what would have been."

Makena was sad he'd had to go through that. But at the same time, she empathized with his ex. It wasn't an easy choice to make. This meant that, to ensure she was never in a position to think about it, she had to take the necessary measures. She would get on contraceptives as soon as possible, that is, if David still wanted them to date. As she'd sat in the bathroom waiting for the test results, she'd decided that whatever happened, she wanted to be with him. It wouldn't be easy, but she knew she could trust him. She would enjoy this, live in this moment, for as long as she could.

"I'm sorry that happened to you, and as you said, it must have been hard for her. I respect you for not guilting her or abandoning her," she said. "I want you to know that while I'm not sure what choice I would have made in the same situation when I thought I was pregnant, I was scared, but the idea of having your baby didn't completely horrify me. That said, I agree with you that we should do whatever it takes to ensure this doesn't happen until we're ready."

"So you're saying yes, to us dating?" he asked, hopefully.

She leaned in and pulled him into a sensuous kiss, and then she pulled back and nodded.

"Good. You have no idea how much I have missed you. But I'll show you."

They spent hours on the couch, kissing and talking. He put a movie on the large flatscreen TV, but they barely followed, so he put on some music. He brought a bottle of wine and a glass for her. He ordered food for them when she mentioned she hadn't eaten all day. She had shown up at his house at eight p.m. so he must have assumed she'd already eaten.

"What are you and Gerald doing tomorrow?"

Makena relayed she didn't have any plans—she wanted to spend some more time with Julia and the baby before the work week started.

"Can I take Gerald? I can bring him here, and he can play video games. Plus the building has a swimming pool on the rooftop. He told me he likes swimming."

She thought about it for a while.

"If you're not ready for him to know we're dating, I won't tell him," David continued. "I just want you to know that it's not just the two of us in this, he's also included. You're a package deal for me. I'm here for him, too. You can count on me to take care of the both of you, and I want him to know it, too."

"Okay," she said. "But I really would prefer we keep the fact that we're dating to ourselves, at least for now. But you've spent time with him so he won't find it strange. Also, he loves video games. His favourites are Mario Kart and Sonic."

"Thanks for telling me. We'll have a lot of fun."

"Don't feed him a lot of junk food or let him drink any soda. Juice is okay, but soda goes right to his head and also gives him tonsilitis sometimes. Nothing straight out of the fridge, and if you're going to the pool, watch him at all times."

"Okay, mama bear. Would you care to write all that down?" he joked.

"David," she started in a serious tone. "I have no sense of humour when it comes to my only child."

He held her all night, and no matter how much they both wanted it, they didn't attempt to make love. She slept in his shirt and underwear, and he slept in pyjama bottoms. She was awake for hours, alternating between the thrill of the shift in their relationship and the nervousness over how long it would last. Several times, she thought about telling him about Paul, but she couldn't bring herself to. She would lose him, and worst of all, she couldn't stand for him to pity her. The way he saw her was as an attractive, badass single mum who was doing whatever it takes to raise a wonderful little boy. This was something she never wanted to lose.

Chapter Ten

Makena got to the hospital just in time for lunch hour visiting time. She'd brought some clothes she had bought for the baby and had cooked her friend some chicken stew. Julia was thrilled at the homemade food. Henry had dropped by in the morning and left when she arrived.

"How's it going?" she asked as she held Lily.

"So far, so good. Once I got over the excruciating pain when she breastfeeds. I can't get over how beautiful and little she is. Maybe I'm biased because I'm her mother, but God, she smells so good," Julia said, sighing in contentment.

"You're not biased. She's so adorable. And quiet. Did she fuss at night?"

"Surprisingly, no. The nurses had warned me that she would be up several times at night, but she wasn't. I woke her up to feed her. At some point, I was worried she wasn't okay, but they told me I should count myself lucky."

"You should. As you may remember, I was a zombie the first six months of Gerald's life. I barely slept."

"And now, he's a big boy," Julia said.

Makena's eyes filled with a twinge of nostalgia as she sniffed Lily's head which was covered in a lime green hat.

"Stop, what's happening to your face? Do you want another baby? Are you having baby fever?"

"What? No!" When Julia sighed in disbelief, she continued, "Fine. Yesterday when I left, it was to take a pregnancy test. I'm not pregnant, but I had reason to suspect I might be." She sat down on the chair and told Julia everything.

"So you have been sleeping with David for months and now you're dating?" Julia asked in surprise.

"Yes. I couldn't tell you because there wasn't anything to tell, until yesterday. The thing is, I didn't absolutely hate the idea of having another baby. I've never given much thought to having another child, and I'm still not sure about it, but he was great when I told him I could be pregnant."

"That's because you hadn't been in love. You've seen how he is with Gerald and his niece and nephew. I'm sure that must have reassured you."

"Gerald loves him. He did even when I didn't care for him at all. I wouldn't even have considered getting into a relationship with him if Gerald disliked him."

Julia got serious all of a sudden. "What about Paul? What will you do if he finds you?"

"Probably the same thing I've always done. I just want to stop and take a breath before that happens. I've earned it," Makena said, her voice catching. She didn't want to talk about him.

"Yes, you have," Julia said.

They talked some more about how Julia was dealing with being a new mum. Makena held the baby while she showered. The baby woke up and cried a little, but she was able to calm her down by rocking her for a bit. She texted David to see how they were doing, and he replied to tell her they were knee-deep in a Sonic game which Gerald was winning.

SHE WENT TO DAVID'S after she left late in the afternoon. Gerald was so comfortable with him. He loved the giant TV mounted to the wall. He alternated between playing games and watching cartoons. David had ordered pizza for lunch. They had even had a dip in the pool which Gerald was thrilled about. He asked whether they could move in. Makena shook her head, and David said they couldn't because it was too far from school but they could visit whenever he wanted. She took advantage of his magnificent well-equipped kitchen to make them vegetable rice and mutton stew.

"This is amazing, thank you," David said after he had wiped his plate clean.

Gerald, as usual, took the time to remove all the bell peppers before eating his food.

"You're welcome," she said.

They were seated on the couch while Gerald sat on the carpet. David collected the dishes and cleaned them. He then joined her on the couch, and she lay her feet on his thighs. Gerald was fascinated by whatever was going on on the TV and didn't bother them.

"I like this," David said. "There's an extra bedroom for when you want to visit with him. Then you won't have to worry about finding someone to babysit him. Maybe even move in?"

"First of all, thanks for the offer. We could visit for a weekend. But no to moving in. It's way too soon, and I have a job which would make for an unreasonable commute."

David seemed to give it some thought and then agreed with her. She rewarded him with a quick peck on the lips. They both glanced at Gerald knowing that's the most they could do.

"What's your dream job?" he asked.

"Well, before I went to college for social work, the plan was to get my degree immediately after and then look for a job either in the children's department in the government or an NGO dealing with women and children's welfare," she said.

"Why didn't you do that?"

"I had a baby and got busy making a home. After my relationship ended, I didn't know whether that was in the cards for me. I never put down roots long enough to go to school or get my dream job."

"But when we met, you told me that you kept moving because of work."

She was surprised he remembered, but even more importantly, he implied he had caught her in a lie, which he had.

"That was part of it. There were other factors that I can't talk about now," she said with a tone of finality, leaving no room for further inquiry. "Anyway, I'm thinking of getting my degree next year. I've been doing some research, and I can make it work. I'll study virtually in case we have to move again."

"That's a great idea, and I can help you if you need any help," he said.

She would never accept any financial help from him, but she didn't bring it up.

"What's your dream job?" she asked him.

"I already told you, CFO. Thankfully, I have the academic qualifications. I wouldn't be caught dead in a classroom again," he said with a laugh.

She threw a pillow at him for making fun of her impending future as a student. He caught it and threw it back.

When Gerald started indicating he was sleepy, David drove them home. The boy promptly fell asleep on the back seat.

"Your mum told me about her party next Saturday. She invited me, and I couldn't get out of it," Makena said.

"Why would you want to get out of it? She loves you."

"At the time, you and I had barely talked, and I thought it would be awkward since we were done."

"You and I will never be done. When we're ready, we will tell her, and I'm sure she will be thrilled." He stole a glimpse at her. "She really does love you. Has she ever done anything to make you feel otherwise?"

"No, but then again, I'm the person who dispenses her medication." She chuckled. "This isn't just an ordinary boyfriend's mum. I'm her employee, not to mention the little package at the back. Most mothers aren't keen on girlfriends who have an extra package."

"I don't know what I can do to alleviate your fears other than to say I'll wait to tell her until you're ready. Don't worry about it," he said. "Will you be at the party? It's really small, not more than thirty people. Her friends from church and some of our aunts and uncles."

That didn't reassure her, but she nodded.

They arrived, and he helped her get Gerald into their house. When he was safely tucked in, David kissed her goodnight and left. He would be spending the night in the main house rather than going back to his apartment.

AS HE HAD TOLD HER, his mother's birthday was a small event. Makena got to meet some of his aunts, and they liked her. Everyone liked her because they seemed convinced she was the only thing keeping Mrs. Mutua alive even though she didn't think so herself.

The party was held in the backyard garden. She tried to help the caterers, but every time Mrs. Mutua or Allison saw her, they would stop her. She didn't like not having something to do. For the party, she wore a cream skater dress that reached below the knee and accentuated her waist and upper half. She coupled it with brown sandals and minimal jewellery. Gerald, Gianna, and Nathan were the only kids at the party. They were allowed to play around and watch TV so long as they didn't get underfoot. Allison's nanny was watching them.

The minute she walked into the party, she felt David's eyes on her. She couldn't dare look at him because she feared if she did, she would falter, or her feelings for him would be written on her face for all to see. She took a seat at the back, and only when she was fully settled did she raise her head to look at the front where David, Allison, her husband, and their mother were seated.

Her gaze collided with his, and she felt her face heat up. He smiled and winked at her, and she nearly came undone. It was all she could do to nod at him. Once the buffet was laid out, one of David's aunts prayed for the food, and people started serving. Makena got up to get Mrs. Mutua's food. She went to the kitchen because she had instructed the caterers to make her separate food aligning with her dietary needs. She prepared a plate and brought it to her.

"Makena, I told you, you're a guest today," Mrs. Mutua protested as she brought her the plate and a bottle of water.

"I'm just making sure you eat right. I promise not to lift a finger after this," she said with a chuckle.

"I don't believe you, but Allison, just in case she tries, see to it that she doesn't," Mrs. Mutua said to her daughter. Allison nodded in agreement. "Good, now go get yourself something to eat, and don't worry about your boy at all, he's well taken care of."

She got herself a plate of food and returned to her seat. Everyone was talking amongst themselves, leaving her out of place as the only people she knew at the party were at the high table. Once she was done, she took her plate to the kitchen where the cleanup was taking place. She checked in on the kids and then dashed to her house to apply some lipstick.

She was barely inside when the door opened. She turned to see David. He had dressed in a navy-blue suit minus the tie with the top button of his white shirt undone. She fought her body's reaction to him and raised her hand, but he stepped towards her, and it landed on his chest. She could feel his heart beating.

"You shouldn't be here. This isn't how we hide this from your family," she said.

"I missed you."

He laid his hand on her waist and pulled her closer to him—so close, she could feel his breath on her face. It was delicious. She closed her eyes and took it in, and she parted her lips. When he finally brought his lips to hers, she could barely breathe. With his lips, he coaxed her to open up, and she did, letting him consume her. She could taste the hint of peppermint from his mouthwash, but more than that, she could taste him, all masculine, intoxicating, and all-consuming. They were making love with just their mouths, and by the time he let her go, she drew in a deep breath to fill in her deprived lungs.

"I missed you, too," she said.

She passed her tongue over her lips for a quick check because she was convinced they were swollen. She couldn't believe she had come out of that kiss unscathed, not while her whole body tingled with wanting. If he wanted to take her to bed, she wouldn't resist, not even with his whole family outside. But he didn't.

"Good," he said instead, then he straightened his suit and went back out.

Makena stood dazed for a long time. Then forgetting the reason why she came back to her house, she grabbed her phone and went back out.

Allison was waiting for her at the entrance to the main house where she was going. She took her hand and led her to one of the upstairs bedrooms.

"What's going on between you and my brother?"

Makena was stunned by her inquiry and straightforwardness.

"What? Nothing is happening, we're just friends."

"Makena, I'm not angry or trying to get you fired, trust me. I've had my suspicions since Gianna's birthday party. Then today, he followed you to your house and came out looking...well, I can't even say. And you waited the standard five minutes to avoid suspicion."

She hadn't even been thinking about that.

"Allison, David is my friend, and if anything was happening between us, it wouldn't be my place to tell you. If it was happening, it wouldn't affect my duties or my ability to take care of your mum, rest assured."

She didn't want Allison to peg her as a dumb bimbo who banged her boss's son and reneged on her duties.

"I know that. Your ability to do your job is not in question. I'm concerned that when David breaks your heart, you won't want to work for our mother anymore, which we would all be devastated about."

She was surprised by how little faith Allison had in her brother. Allison seemed confident he would break her heart, but Makena knew he wouldn't. If anything, she would be the one who bailed on their relationship.

"Allison, I appreciate your concern. But as I said, I will keep my work and personal life separate. If I date someone, it won't affect my job."

Allison nodded and didn't ask her anything else. She went back to the party, and Makena joined the kids for a while. The way she had been brought down from the sexual high of David's kiss to being made to answer to his sister shook her. She needed to step away from the situation for a while, and the childish chatter of the children was exactly what she needed.

They had already eaten and were now playing games on Gianna's phone. They played so well together, none of them was hoarding the phone. They had never stayed anywhere long enough for Gerald to create such rapport with the kids. Lily was too young, and their relationship would probably be that of a protective older brother with his baby sister. If Makena had a choice on who she wanted her son to grow up around, Gianna and Nathan would top the list. They were lovely, polite, and despite growing up wealthy, they were well-disciplined.

Allison came to get them for the cake-cutting, shaking her from her thoughts. She got the cake and had the three kids follow her, singing happy birthday. They took photos of Mrs. Mutua cutting the cake with the children, then she gave each of them a piece and then David and Allison. Makena was surprised when she called her up, as well. She introduced herself and then gave her a slice of cake. She ate a small piece herself.

Later, she helped with the cleanup, and when the catering vans were gone, she headed for her house. David followed her in.

"Are you okay?" he asked as soon as they were inside.

"Yeah, I'm fine, just a bit tired. I'll go get Gerald later. I don't want to pull him away just yet," she said, withdrawing from him.

She sat on the sofa, and he joined her, though she barely looked at him.

"I'm sorry about what Allison said to you. She had no business interrogating you like that."

She looked at him, surprised. "What? She told you?"

"Yeah. She's not a total bitch. I gave her a serious talk about poking her nose in other people's business." He took her hand so she wouldn't turn away from him.

"Great, and now she knows for sure that there's something between us." Makena sighed in defeat. This was the last thing she wanted.

"Makena, she's a lawyer. You didn't fool her one bit with all the deflecting," he said. "In return for being a nosy sister, Allison said since she's spending the night, as is her nanny, my mum and Gerald will be taken care of. So you and I can have some alone time."

Makena stood up and walked to the bedroom. She struggled to unzip her dress only for David to set her hands aside and do it himself. His hands lingered on her naked flesh, sending goosebumps all over her skin.

"I don't think I should. If Allison is having concerns about our relationship affecting my job, wouldn't my going off with you just reinforce her theory? Besides, I want to stay here, cosy up on the couch, and watch some *Muchacha Italiana*."

David was silent for a while. He pressed his thumbs on the back of her neck and rubbed circles in a gentle massage. She leaned into it.

"Are you sure? Because I was looking forward to having you in my apartment. I want to make love to you in all five rooms. I want to wake up next to you, for us to have breakfast together. If that doesn't entice you, how about cuddling with me on the couch as you watch *Muchacha*? I make the best buttered popcorn."

"Seven," she said, then sighed as he started to slide her dress down her shoulders. "You said five rooms. Your house has seven. You forgot the bathrooms."

"Actually, I forgot one bathroom. We can't make love in one of the bedrooms, it's forbidden. If you're curious about it, you'll have to come with me."

She stepped out of the dress and turned around to face him. She wore only a pink lacy bra and black panties. David sighed in appreciation. She walked out of his grasp, teasing him.

"Fine, I will think about coming, but only because you have an eighty-inch TV, and I'm curious about that bedroom. My mind is running wild. I shouldn't have read *Fifty Shades of Grey*. Also, I need to speak to Allison myself and also Gerald to make sure he's fine with me. leaving. I feel like I have been abandoning him too much."

She went to the wardrobe and pulled out black pants, a white shirt, a blue dress, and some underwear. She packed the dress, underwear, and toiletries in a bag and handed it to him. "Take that to your car. I'll get dressed."

Chapter Eleven

"What did you tell Allison?" David asked on the drive to his house.

They had lingered long enough to help his mother say goodbye to her guests and for Makena to say goodbye to Gerald who seemed completely unfazed by his mother's absence for the second weekend in a row.

"None of your business," she answered.

Her talk with Allison had been much more pleasant than she had anticipated. Allison apologized for butting in and assured her she wanted some alone time with her mum and would take care of everything. Allison had been Mrs. Mutua's caregiver for a while after she left the hospital before they started hiring professionals, so she knew what she was doing. She also promised to keep her knowledge of their relationship to herself.

"Technically, it is my business, but okay," he said.

When they got to his house, they stored the leftovers his mother had packed for him in the fridge. Then he led her to one of the guest bedrooms. When he had given her a tour of the house the previous weekend, one of the bedrooms had been converted into a home office and the other had been empty.

In the week since she'd last seen it, it had been completely transformed into a boy's dream bedroom. It had a single bed covered in a black and blue duvet. There was a poster of Black Panther hanging above the headboard—he was Gerald's favourite superhero. In one corner of the room was a desk and chair and in another, a large blue bean bag. He had put several exercise books, sketching pads, and colouring pens on the desk. There was a football and a toy plane on the floor atop a grey wall-to-wall carpet.

"I wanted to get him a desktop computer, but I thought you wouldn't like that," he said.

Makena was so in awe, she didn't know what to say. She had always dreamed of making Gerald's bedroom just like this when they had a bigger place to live in. She threw her arms around him.

"He is going to love it. Thank you. And thank you for not buying the computer. He's too young for that. When did you do all this?"

"I had a day off, and I went shopping. When Gerald was here last week, I asked him a few things to give me something to work with."

Her eyes misted up at his thoughtfulness. She didn't want him to see her cry, but she couldn't help it.

"So, he gets a whole bedroom, and I don't even have a drawer?" She chuckled.

"You have a whole section of the closet waiting for you. I meant it when I said you can move in if you want. I just wanted to show you that I'm ready whenever you are."

She raised on tiptoes and kissed him. He ground his body against hers, and she felt him harden in response. She dragged her lips away from his.

"If you meant it, about not making love here, we better take it elsewhere. And by the way, I'll make you pay for letting me make *Fifty Shades of Grey* references about my son's new bedroom."

"Hey, I can't be blamed for your dirty mind." He kissed her again and led her to his office which was between the two bedrooms. "I look forward to the new image on my desk."

She sat on the desk. He stood between her legs and held her face in his hands. She spread her hands on the surface and lifted herself to reach his lips, kissing him deeply. He reached for her shirt and pulled it over her head, pausing the kiss long enough to take it off. She unbuttoned his shirt and pulled it from his pants, then undid his belt. His lips left hers and descended to her neck where he kissed a sweet spot that sent a jolt of feeling all the way to her core. He undid her bra and pulled it off then started caressing her boobs, landing soft touches on her nipples with her thumbs.

"I missed these," he said roughly.

Makena unbuttoned his pants and carefully lowered the zipper over his boxers which covered his erection. Then, she dipped her hand into his boxers and pulled out his dick. She wrapped her palm around him and pumped gently, eliciting a moan. He stepped back and made quick work of her pants and underwear, leaving her ass sitting bare on the cold surface of his desk. He brought his fingers to her wet centre, dipping one in while another played with her clit. She kept working his dick as he worked her opening, driving her crazy as she knew she was doing to him.

"I want you inside me, now," she said as her orgasm drew close. She wanted him inside her when it hit her.

He opened a drawer on the desk and handed her a condom. She opened the foil package and wrapped his erection in the condom. She rubbed his head on her wet opening, teasing herself and him wantonly.

"No more playing," David said between gritted teeth as he pulled away from her hand and held her buttocks. He pushed inside her hard, bottoming out. He took her hard and fast. "I need you like this. I promise we'll go slow next time."

Still, she felt her release taking her over, quickly overcoming her just as it had when he'd been touching her. He lowered his mouth on her nipple and bit lightly, taking her over the edge. She held him tightly as she rode the wave, feeling him twitch and release inside her.

They held each other for long minutes, breathing heavily. When she could finally speak, she said, "I love your desk."

He laughed as he pulled out of her. "Now, so do I."

MAKENA FELT LIKE SHE was riding a cloud of happiness as the week started. It was also Gerald's birthday week, so she had double reason for happiness. She woke up early Monday morning and made him fluffy pancakes for breakfast. His birthday was on Thursday, and as she did every year, she would spend the week doing his favourite things. Gerald was usually thrilled by the effort. She walked him to school and even let him go without a hug, which for him meant she didn't embarrass him.

"Hello, Mama Gerald," Ricky greeted from behind her.

She turned around to face him.

"Hello, Baba Jack. I have to go."

"Look, I realize I may have been a little harsh last time, but you were playing hard to get unnecessarily. All while bunking up with your rich boss's son."

Makena did all she could not to roll her eyes at his non-apology.

"Kids talk," he continued. "Which reminds me, tell your son a happy birthday. I hear he turns nine this week. Also, tell him his daddy says hi. Paul was thrilled to hear how well you're both doing."

He turned around and walked off. Makena nearly ran home because she was panicking, and she needed to hold it together until she was safely inside the house. The gateman looked at her strangely when she didn't stop to say hi. Once she was inside the house, she tried to process what Ricky had said.

What if he had found Paul and planned to set him on her because she had rejected him? Everything she had built here, her son's happiness, it was all going to fall apart. If he found her, she couldn't stay. She would have to take her son and run.

She grabbed her phone and checked her messages. There was nothing from Paul. He usually texted her to rile her up first whenever he found them. Maybe there was no cause for concern. Ricky had said kids talk, so maybe Gerald had mentioned Paul's name to Jack who had, in turn, told his father.

She tried not to let it ruin Gerald's birthday week. While she was subdued for most of the week, she still managed to make it special for him. She picked him up from school as a means of extra precaution. She had contemplated telling Julia to pick her brain, but she didn't want to bother her because of the baby.

She also couldn't tell David because she hadn't told him anything about Paul. She wouldn't know where to begin. She didn't want him to ever know about her past. When they talked, she tried to hide her growing sense of apprehension, and she must have done it well enough because he didn't question her on it.

Every time she got a text message, she felt a sense of dread. She hadn't run into Ricky again, and she hadn't gotten anything from Paul. By the time Thursday arrived, she was starting to believe Ricky was bluffing.

For Gerald's birthday, she had gotten permission from his teacher to bring a birthday cake to the class during break time. They had finished their end-of-term exams the day before and were just waiting for the results and closing date. This way, his whole class got to celebrate with him. Gerald was popular amongst his classmates, and he was thrilled by the idea. She ordered a lemon cake from Valentine's and bought some snacks and party hats. It was a minimalist birthday which allowed her to stay on budget.

After serving Mrs. Mutua lunch, she walked to Gerald's school. David had asked whether he could come, but she didn't want him to get out of work. She also wanted it to be just her and Gerald, not wanting their relationship to overshadow his day.

Gerald took pride in sharing the cake with the whole class. He was beaming as he introduced Makena to every one of his classmates. When they were done, they gave the teacher the remainder of the cake to take home.

Just as they were about to leave, there was a knock on the door.

"Is this Gerald's class? I'm here to wish him a happy birthday."

Makena froze, and a lump filled her throat, making it hard to swallow. She fought the rising panic, and even though she was nowhere near the door, she took several steps to get even farther away. She grabbed Gerald and pushed him behind her.

"And who are you?" she heard the teacher ask.

But she knew the answer already.

"I'm his father," Paul responded.

She hadn't heard that voice in five years. The last time she had seen his face, he had been raining blows on her. She was paralysed. All she wanted was to keep her son safe, but she couldn't move an inch.

"We need to get out of here," she whispered. By then, Paul had made his way into the class. "Go get your bag, Gerald."

She let the teacher know they were leaving without raising alarm with the rest of the class. Makena took Gerald's hand firmly as soon as he had his things and walked towards the door. She stopped in front of Paul. Her heart was beating fast as she stood and faced him.

"I'm not letting you anywhere near my son," she said, and without giving him time to respond, quickly walked out of the class and towards the gate.

As soon as they were out, she started jogging. Gerald followed her lead. When they got to the gate, she asked the gateman not to let anyone in as they were being followed. He nodded, eyeing her with concern.

She took Gerald's hand and led him to their house, where she asked him to change out of his school uniform. She hastily packed a small suitcase with as much of her clothes as she could fit in. Then, she texted Julia letting her know Paul had found them and asking if they could come stay with her for a few days. Julia quickly responded in the affirmative and asked if they were okay.

Makena didn't text back. Whatever energy she had left, she wanted to expend it on things that mattered. If she allowed herself to feel anything right now, she would fall apart, and she couldn't do that.

She didn't hear Gerald walk into the bedroom.

"Mum, are we leaving again?"

"Yes, my angel. I'm sorry, but we can't stay here anymore." She could see him fighting tears. She wanted more than anything to comfort him, but she couldn't do that without allowing herself to feel the despair of the situation. "Go say goodbye to Mrs. Mutua."

When Gerald was gone, she took another bag and packed up some of his clothes. She took a paper bag and put in several pairs of their shoes and Gerald's roller skates. Everything else, she would have to collect later. She couldn't bring herself to go to Mrs. Mutua, so she called the maid and let her know she was leaving and gave her instructions on what to cook for supper. Once she was safely at Julia's, she would reach out to Allison. She wouldn't be talking to David anymore—whatever relationship she'd been attempting to build with him was gone. Destroyed by the sudden reappearance of her ex.

She called her usual bodaboda guy, and he arrived in ten minutes. She and Gerald climbed on, and as they rode towards the main road, she watched everything they were leaving behind. Gerald was wedged between her and the rider, his hands gripping the rider's jacket tightly.

As they left the smooth tarmacked road of the estate and joined the other part of the small town, the road got rough and bumpy. She covered her son's hands with her own. They were warm, a contrast to her cold ones. She felt as if her heart was pumping ice all over her body. Her gaze darted around the road. When they arrived at the matatu stage, she quickly paid the rider, and they got into a matatu.

Every time the conductor banged on the side to try and get more passengers, Makena's heart somersaulted in her chest. She looked behind them, but she wouldn't even know which car was Paul's if he was following them.

It was a short ride to the next stop where Henry would pick them up. She texted Julia to let her know they were on the way. Gerald had laid his head on her shoulder, and he was crying silently. He was blinking hard to keep the tears from falling, but they fell anyway, so he pulled at the sleeve of his sweater and wiped them away. Makena patted his head, lost at what she could say to comfort her son. The matatu stopped, and they had to alight. By then, Gerald had composed himself.

Henry's car was parked next to the matatu stage. She took their bags and put them in the boot. They didn't say anything on the short drive home. She sat at the back with Gerald in case he was distressed, but he was no longer crying. She gave him her phone to play games with.

Julia was waiting on the step outside the two-story house. She started to hug her, but Makena put her hand up to halt her, so she hugged Gerald and led him inside by the shoulder. She followed silently. The nanny was seated on the couch rocking Lily. Julia asked Gerald to stay in the living room and went with Makena to the guest room on the ground floor.

"Tell me what happened," she said when they were seated on the bed.

"What's there to tell? He found us, and we had to leave."

"How are you?"

"I don't know. I haven't stopped to think about anything since I saw him. I haven't seen him since that day, Julia. I can't think about it right now."

But even as she said that, the corners of her eyes started to darken, and the vision of what was in front of her, the calming blue of the wall, blurred. In her mind's eye, she saw Paul as he was today. He wore his police uniform, probably meaning to intimidate her or to ensure he got access to the school. She started sweating and breathing fast. She slid onto the floor and placed both her hands on the cool tiles, but the cold did nothing to stop the flush of heat. She tried to fight the darkness, trying the breathing exercises she had learnt over the years, but she couldn't concentrate.

"Julia, I... I can't..."

The words refused to come out. Julia tried to talk her through it, but she started hyperventilating. Tears rolled down her cheeks, and she couldn't hear what Julia was saying. From a distance, she heard her talking, but it was all muffled.

She lay down on the floor and closed her eyes, wanting to ride it out. Once again, she had let the person she loved the most down—she could see Gerald crying as they rode in the matatu. And David, they were done; they couldn't be together. She would always be alone, but not alone because she would always have her baby, who she would always let down. More tears gathered at the corners of her eyes.

It seemed like it lasted hours, but only twenty minutes had passed. Julia was lying next to her on the floor. She was as close to her as she could be without touching her. This wasn't the first time she had been with her in the throes of a panic attack so she knew the drill.

"You're okay now," she said.

"No, I'm not. I'm a mess. I can't keep running to you when there's trouble. You have an actual baby now," Makena said, quickly sitting up. She wiped her tears with the back of her hand.

"Yes, you can. My baby has me, a supportive father, and an amazing nanny, and you have me. I'm not bragging. I'm just letting you know that I will always have time for you. You and Gerald can stay with me for as long as you need."

Makena climbed on the bed and lay down.

"We can't. I appreciate the offer, and I know you mean it. But we can't stay here indefinitely. I have to start looking for another job in another town, another place to live, another school for Gerald."

Julia didn't say anything. Makena had been through this several times. Most of the time, she was all alone. She gave herself two days. She would go back to Mrs. Mutua's the next day to pack her things, then the day after, she would be gone.

"What about David?" Julia asked.

"That's over. We can't be together while I'm running for my life," she answered, the remorse all over her low voice. "I have to go see Gerald. He's having a hard time with this."

She joined Gerald in the living room, and he handed her back her phone.

"Uncle David called. He asked where we were," he said. "I told him we were going away."

Makena's heart skipped a beat. She wasn't ready to have a conversation with David. Before she could contemplate what to do, her phone rang again. She decided to pick up his call rather than ignore it and hope he would go away. She went outside and sat on the bench in the front yard.

"Hello, David," she said, her voice shaking.

"What happened? Where are you?" he asked, foregoing pleasantries.

"We left. I can't do this anymore. I was going to call Allison about quitting my job, and I made sure your mum will be well taken care of today while you make arrangements. I will come to get my things as soon as I can," she said, keeping her voice as steady as she could.

"So you left your job just like that? One minute, we're making plans for the weekend, and now, you're gone, with no explanation? Were you even going to call me?"

She said nothing.

"What happened at the party?" he asked. "The gateman said you ran home from Gerald's school, and when we talked this morning, everything was fine. What happened at the party?"

"Nothing happened. It was just time to leave."

"Stop lying," he said forcefully. She heard him take a deep breath. "You're at Julia's, right? You didn't pack enough to get further. I'm coming. If you're going to abandon me, you will do it in person. Send me the location, or I will have to ask around. Either way, I will find out where you are."

Makena hung up the phone. David was determined—she didn't doubt he would find her. She would have to break up with him in person, and it terrified her. She sent him the location pin on WhatsApp. He opened the message immediately. She buried her face in her hands, then went back to the house to sit with Gerald. He seemed calmer now and was engrossed in a game of Tetris on the TV. Makena knew she would have to have a conversation with him, but it would come later when she had more details.

Less than twenty minutes later, there was a honk at the gate. Henry went to open it and let David in.

He came barrelling inside, and when he saw her, she was ready for him to yell at her. Instead, he pulled her into a hug and held her tightly in his arms. She blinked away the tears threatening to overflow from her eyes.

"Don't you ever do that to me again," he whispered in her ear then released her. He turned to Gerald and gave him a fist bump, and for the first time since they'd left, her boy smiled. She felt her heart clench as if held in a vise-like grip.

"We need to talk," she said, her lip shaking. She took his hand and led him outside to the bench she was occupying earlier.

"What happened at the party? I want the truth, no walk around or lies. Why did you leave without telling anyone?"

"My ex, Gerald's father, showed up at the party. That means he knows where we are, and we had to leave immediately. I couldn't take a minute to call anyone. I just had to get my son away," she said earnestly.

David looked at her in shock, his eyes narrowing.

"I thought you were attacked or something. So you put us through all this because Gerald's father wanted to see his son on his birthday? I know you're not in touch, but isn't that a good thing?" He raised his hand to scratch his head, and Makena instinctively flinched. He dropped it instantly. "Are you afraid of me?"

"No…" she said nervously. "You were so angry when you called and just now. Anyway, I need to tell you something about my ex. I didn't just leave him. I ran, and there's a reason why I run every time he finds us."

"Did he hurt you?" David asked, gripping the chair.

Makena saw this and instinctively wanted to reach out and cover his hand with hers. She stopped herself and looked away from him.

"He was abusive, not just physically, but also emotionally. When he hurt Gerald during one of our fights, I had to leave."

David reached out to hold her. She put her hands up to stop him and moved away.

"When he showed up today, it was the first time I had seen him since we left. Whenever he finds out where we are, he sends a message, threatens me. But this time, he showed up."

Davids's eye shifted to the scar on her hand. She had a few more, but that was the only one he had ever commented on. She had quickly deflected, and he'd probably assumed the rest of the scars were a result of being clumsy as she had said.

"Your scars," he said. "I'm an idiot for never figuring it out. It's what people say, that they fell or they were clumsy."

"I didn't tell you or make the implication. I never expected you to just figure it out."

"I understand the need to run, but were you ever going to call me?"

She shook her head. "I love you, David, but if I stayed, I would have put your family in danger, and I would never do that to you. I love you very much, but you and I can't be together anymore. I have to find somewhere else to go. You have to go, I'm sorry."

She captured his face in her hands and gave him a tender kiss. The tears that had been threatening all day ran down her cheeks. Her heart ached, and the lump in her throat grew tenfold. She released him and stood up.

"No," he said, taking her hand gently. She refused to turn to face him. "You can't tell me you love me and then ask me to leave. Why would you do that? I can keep you safe. Come home with me."

Makena sat back down. She wiped the tears with the back of her hand. She fidgeted with her hands, the indecision evident in her gestures.

"There's a bedroom for Gerald in my apartment. Besides, I'm not leaving without you. Think about it, Makena. I live far from my mum's, and if you stay here, it's likely the first place he will come looking."

David was right. At the other times, staying with Julia hadn't been an option because she'd been far away. But this time, she was close, so Paul would come to the same conclusion she had, that she had gone to Julia's. Leaving David was one of the hardest things she'd ever had to do. Her chest tightened at the thought that she could never see him again.

"I don't want to bring the mess to your life. I need to get out of town," she said, shaking her head. She could feel herself wavering.

"You must not have heard me, Makena. I said I'm not leaving you and Gerald here." His jaw clenched with the effort to maintain composure.

She nodded, then went back into the house. He waited with Gerald as she went to get their bags. Julia followed her. She wanted reassurance she was sure about what she was doing. David packed their bags in the boot of his car and waited for them to say goodbye. He had promised Julia he would take good care of them. Makena promised to call and text, and they left.

"Why didn't Charlie help you? He never mentioned any of it to me," he asked when they were on the road.

"I never told him. When I left, all I told him was that things hadn't worked out."

"All this time, you let him think you're a screwup who can't hold down a job. Why?" he asked, puzzled.

"He came to that conclusion on his own. I only asked for his help a few times. I would just let him know when I moved because he's family. I didn't even ask him for this job, but the terms were good enough so I took it." She had been disappointed to learn what her brother thought of her, and she hadn't spoken to him since. He had texted a few times, but she'd let the messages go unanswered.

"I'm sorry this happened to you, and that you feel you have to take care of everything by yourself. But you don't have to anymore. I'm here now. I told you that I'm here for you and Gerald. I meant it. I'm disappointed that you didn't have enough faith in me, in us, to let me in on this. You and Gerald will be safe at my house and everywhere you go. I will make sure of that."

She nodded.

"I'm sorry I didn't tell you any of this. The only person who knew was Julia, and I felt it was easier to just turn to her. She was there when things were really bad, and then I was alone for so long. This relationship between us, it's something I wouldn't have anticipated. I didn't plan for it, and I don't know how to deal with it."

David took her hand and kissed it. She had told him she loved him, and he hadn't responded. She knew him enough to understand he wasn't the kind of man to make empty declarations. So his lack of a response didn't bother her that much. The way he had swung into action today, offering her and her son a home, listening to her without judgment—she loved him more for all it.

Chapter Twelve

Makena woke up the next morning with her face buried in David's chest. His eyes were closed, and he was snoring lightly. She reached out to touch his face then stilled, not wanting to wake him up. They had been talking until late into the night. She didn't know whether he would be going to work. It was almost seven a.m. Since she was used to waking up early, she couldn't sleep any more. She quietly got out of bed and went to the washroom. When she was done, she put on a pair of tights. She had slept in David's shirt and hadn't bothered to unpack her things.

She went to the kitchen to see if there was anything she could make for breakfast. She made tea and toast. She was hungry since she hadn't had supper the previous night. She also made herself some eggs and would make David and Gerald some when they woke up so the food didn't get cold. She poured the tea into a thermos flask after pouring herself a cup and went to the living room where she found texts from Julia which she responded to, promising to call her later. There was still nothing from Paul.

She was worried about his next move. His showing up had disconcerted her, and she didn't know what he would do next. She was in a different county now, although not that far from where he had found her, but she considered herself safe. David's building had stringent security, and he had assured her several times they would be protected.

Now, she had to figure out what to do next. Top of her list was finding a new job. Living with David provided them with a charmed life, however, she preferred to be working and pulling her weight, or at least some of it. The December holiday was coming up for Gerald so she had time to think about what to do for his schooling. Chances were he would have to transfer if they lived here.

Loving David had changed her. By now, she would've been halfway across the country, terrified but still doing what needed to be done. Being with him had allowed her to pause, and now, she was thinking about whether it wouldn't be better to fight. It would be crazy to think she could win against Paul. If showing up at the police station bruised and beaten hadn't gotten her anywhere, she knew for certain nothing would.

She couldn't allow thoughts of what Paul would do next to consume her. If she did, she would never stop shaking in fear. Right now, she had to think about what she did next. She had to talk to David about looking for another job, thus effectively handing in her notice. She had known as soon as things got serious with David that she couldn't continue working for his mum. It was a conflict of interest she didn't want to get into. Her CV had been polished, and she would start sending out applications as soon as possible.

"Good morning," David greeted, kissing her forehead. "I woke up to an empty bed, not what I signed up for."

Makena looked up at him. He was dressed for work in a charcoal grey suit and a light blue shirt.

"Sorry, I woke up early and wasn't sure what time you usually get up. You look so good in a suit. I almost regret not being there to see you get dressed," she said, giving him a onceover.

"Your loss," he said, winking at her. She felt her body heat up with want. "But don't worry. When I come home in the evening, you can have the pleasure of getting me out of it."

"I'll look forward to that," she said. "Do you have time for breakfast? Tea is ready. I'll just toast some bread and make eggs."

"I'd like that, thank you."

She got breakfast ready and brought it to him. David ate quickly, and by the time he was heading for the door, it was eight-thirty a.m. She took his briefcase as he put on his shoes. Just as he was giving her a quick peck goodbye, Gerald came into the room scratching sleep off his eyes. He let out an ew sound at the sight.

"Good morning, Gerald. I'm going to work now. Makena, I'll be a little late coming home since I need to play catch-up for yesterday, and I don't want to work over the weekend. Bye."

She handed him his briefcase and keys, and he left.

"Good morning, my angel. How did you sleep?" she greeted Gerald.

He sat on the couch, still dressed in his pyjamas.

"I slept okay, Mum. I like my room. Is it my room? Uncle David said it is, but I wasn't sure."

"Well, I guess if Uncle David says so, then it's your room. We may have to stay here for a while, so you can get comfortable. I'll go make you some breakfast."

She went into the kitchen, where she beat an egg on a plate with salt and cinnamon and dipped a slice of bread to make French toast.

"Mum," Gerald called. She hadn't even realized he'd joined her in the kitchen. "Why did Dad come to my school? Is that why we had to leave again?"

"I don't know what he wanted, Gerald, but I promise you that I won't let you get hurt ever again. That's why we left. I want to keep you safe, all the time."

She hugged him, and he wrapped his small hands around her. He was still her little boy, and when he was frightened, it was her he went to. She had no doubt seeing his father had shaken him. It may have been almost five years ago, and he may have been just four years old, but one didn't forget the person that broke their hand and put their mother in the hospital for weeks.

"Okay, Mum. Is Uncle David your boyfriend?"

She was surprised by the way he quickly changed the subject. She wasn't prepared to talk about her relationship with David with anyone, much less her son.

"Yes, he is my boyfriend," she said, deciding to be honest. "David asked me to be his girlfriend, and I said yes. I want you to know that even though he is my boyfriend, you and I are still a team. I love you more than anything, and that doesn't change. And David cares about you and understands that you are my number one. Okay?"

"Yes, Mum. Last night, while you were asleep, he cooked for me and let me use his phone to play games. And on Sunday when you went to see Aunt Julia's baby, we swam in the pool and played video games. I think he's cool."

Cool was one of the greatest honours Gerald could bestow, and so far, he'd only given it to her, Julia, and now David.

While he had breakfast and watched TV, she cleaned up. David was good at picking after himself. The master bedroom was already tidied up, as was the office. So she unpacked her stuff. David wasn't kidding—he had left her a whole wardrobe. Even if she had brought all her clothes, it wouldn't have been full. His side of the wardrobe was filled with his suits and shirts. There were also several sweats folded up. She folded whatever needed folding and hung the rest. Then, she emptied her toiletries in a drawer in the master bathroom.

She went to Gerald's bedroom and tidied up and put his clothes in the wardrobe. She took stock of what they had left behind. Gerald's things had suffered the most in the rush. She hadn't brought any of his toys or his bike. She had also left her laptop and yoga mat. She would go back for the stuff later when she was officially quitting her job.

By midday, she was idle, having done everything that needed doing. Just as she was about to check for what to cook for lunch, the house phone rang. It was the receptionist letting her know there was a delivery for her—lunch for her and Gerald. It consisted of mashed potatoes, beef stew, and coleslaw. Gerald hated coleslaw because of the mayonnaise, so she let him eat his food without it. She texted David to thank him for the lunch. He sent a quick text back in acknowledgement and said he was looking forward to coming home in the evening.

After lunch, Gerald wanted to go for a swim, so she obliged. She went with him to watch him. She had never actually been to the rooftop area of the building. It was beautiful, littered with potted plants, hanging lines on one side, and the pool on the other. There were several lounges in the pool area, and it had a wonderful view of the city. She could see all the way to the CBD from there.

She took one of the loungers, and Gerald got into the pool. She knew how to swim, but she didn't do it often. She pulled out her phone and called Julia who picked on the first ring.

"Hello, how are you? Are you okay?" she asked.

"Hi, Julia. Yeah, I'm good. How are you, and Lily?" Makena asked, hoping to steer the conversation away from her.

"We're good. She's such an easy baby. Sleeps a lot, and barely wakes me up at night. Henry is great with her. He's been changing diapers and bathing her. It's amazing to watch," Julia answered happily. "Now, tell me about Paul. Have you heard from him?"

"No, he hasn't called or texted. I keep waiting for that to happen. I can't believe he just showed up and that will be it. Or maybe he thinks I left. I think he knows about David and me. That dad from Gerald's school who has been hitting on me hinted at knowing him earlier this week. He may have told him."

Julia was quiet for a while. Makena heard her sigh.

"What are you going to do? Will you be leaving?"

"I don't know. Honestly, I'm tired of running, and so is my son. Also, I've never had to leave someone behind. I love David." Gerald called her out and splashed water on her. She waved at him and smiled. "But if we're in danger, I will be putting a target on his back by staying with him. So if he finds us here, I might not have a choice."

"I'm so sorry about this," Julia said.

Makena sighed. She didn't want to keep talking about it. She was worried enough thinking about it.

"What is Gerald doing?" Julia asked. "Sounds like he's having fun."

"Swimming. David's building has a swimming pool and a killer view of Nairobi. I can say with confidence that this is the best building I have ever lived in."

"And now, I know Gerald is done with me. No more bribing him with trips to the estate pool after this," Julia said, pretending to be sad.

"Come on, he loves you, although you might be in competition with David's sister Allison. She has two kids who Gerald loves hanging out with. I'll just step aside and watch the battle ," she said with a laugh.

They talked for a while until Lily started fussing and Julia had to go see her. Gerald wasn't getting tired of the water, so Makena started surfing around job sites to see what her options were.

A breeze started coming in a while later, and she practically dragged Gerald away from the pool to prevent him from catching a chill. She texted David that she would be cooking lest he be tempted to send food for supper. He replied that if they needed to buy anything, there was a well-stocked minimart near the building. He said he couldn't wait to come home.

After a shower, they went to the minimart, which was just a hundred meters from the building. Makena bought some stripes and vegetables. She also purchased a bottle of wine and Delmonte juice; she had noticed they didn't have either. She bought some cheesy corn puffs which were Gerald's favourite snack.

She prepared the stripes with sukuma wiki and ugali. She fed Gerald but wanted to wait for David so they could eat together. By eight p.m., Gerald was dozing off. All that swimming had worn him off. He went to bed and left Makena alone watching TV.

David came home just after the nine o'clock news started. His face lit up at the sight of her in a silk nightdress wrapped in a fleece blanket. He placed a paper bag and his briefcase on the table and went to her, pulling her to kiss her deeply. She was thrown by the enthusiastic greeting.

"Gerald asleep?" he asked when he let go of her.

"Yeah, he swam himself to exhaustion."

"I brought you something." He pulled out a bottle of wine from the shopping bag. "I'll go chill this."

"I bought wine, too," she said with a chuckle.

He laughed from the kitchen.

"Great minds think alike. That's not what I meant, though." He came back and pulled something else from the shopping bag and handed it to her.

It was a photo of the three of them with their go-karting gear. Gerald was holding his helmet standing between them beaming. Makena remembered when David had asked someone to take the photo from his phone. It was mounted in a small frame.

"Aww, this is beautiful. I forgot about it," she said, looking at the picture.

"I thought we could put it on the shelf next to the TV."

Her eyes misted at the gesture. David's house only had one other photograph, of his family at his graduation. Adding one of them together with Gerald was his way of saying they were a family. She placed the photo on the shelf as he wanted.

"I love it, thank you," she said. She hugged him, and he held her.

"You're welcome. I'll take a shower first."

"Okay. I'll warm up supper, and we can eat together."

He held her hand and pulled her to him.

"Oh, no, you won't. This morning, promises were made about getting me out of this suit. I've been waiting for it all day."

She followed him to the bedroom and kept the promise she had made him before slipping off her nightdress. They made love in the shower.

Much later, sated and having eaten supper, they sat down to watch a romantic comedy over wine.

"I can't believe I'm watching this. This will ruin my Netflix suggestions for life," he said.

"Hey, you knew what you were signing up for. Now please keep quiet and let's watch Sandra Bullock win Miss Congeniality," she said.

"And what exactly is Miss Congeniality?"

"It's a beauty pageant award which Sandra Bullock's character got for bravery after she— Never mind, I can see your eyes glazing over. Tell me about your day."

David turned his full attention to her. He dropped his phone which he had been planning on using as a distraction while she watched the movie.

"Same old. I put out a few fires in our new branches. I might have to travel to Kigali in the next few weeks, though. How was yours?"

"It was good. I feel much better about things now. I can't thank you enough, not just for giving us a haven, for being there for us." He nodded. "I told Gerald about us. He asked, and I didn't want to lie about it. He seemed okay with it. He said you're cool."

"I know, he told me on Sunday. He liked me way before you did. It's good that you told him. I wouldn't have wanted you to hide it from him. He's a good kid, and he trusts you."

Makena's heart swelled with love for this man. She had had months to observe how he treated Gerald even before they started their relationship. It was one of the things which had drawn her to him. He had never, at any point, acted as if her having a child was a drawback. And the added complication of a dangerous, abusive, obsessed ex hadn't seemed to faze him that much, either.

"I've been thinking, I want to officially quit my job working for your mum and start looking for another one," she said.

"I thought you might. However, I think you should take some time. What if you went back to school instead?"

She shook her head, then turned to face him wearing a serious look on her face.

"I can't do that. I promised myself that I would always work, no matter what. I'll take online classes. It'll probably take a while for me to get a job anyway, a few weeks at least, given that Christmas and New Year's are around the corner. I want to talk to Charlie about selling our parents' land, so I can pay for school with my share."

David started to protest but then seemed to think better of it. Makena was determined to do things her way. She had valid reason to be wary, and he was doing what he could to not add to that.

MAKENA AND DAVID'S idea of domestic bliss made her think she was in a beautiful dream. On Saturday, they slept in. Technically, it wasn't sleep since they had been awake since seven a.m. and got out of bed two hours later. By the time they got to the sitting room, Gerald was awake watching TV. David insisted on making breakfast. He made them banana pancakes which he then slathered with maple syrup. She was pleasantly surprised by how good they tasted, and Gerald was hooked.

David refused to let her do the laundry—he had a cleaning woman coming on Monday. He guilted her by telling her the woman was desperate for the wages, so she would be denying her if she insisted on doing it. For the second day in a long time, she had absolutely nothing to do after doing their dishes. She sat on the lounger on the balcony taking in the morning sun and enjoying a view of the city.

"What are you up to?" David asked, taking the lounger next to her.

"Absolutely nothing." She chuckled.

He laughed. "Good for you. Do you mind if I take Gerald to the ground floor? There's an area where some of the kids skate. I'm sure he'll like meeting them."

She nodded. She didn't want him glued to the screen all day. It was bad for his eyes, and knowing how social Gerald was, he would enjoy it. She felt a twinge of guilt at letting David take care of her son while she basked in the sun. She told herself it wasn't like he was an infant. As soon as he got to know the other kids, he could go play with them by himself with no supervision.

She whipped up leftovers from the fridge for lunch, and when Gerald and David came back, they ate together. Gerald had made a few friends and asked if he could go play with them in the afternoon. David assured her the gate was always locked and no non-residents were allowed in without express permission from whoever they were visiting. Gerald swore not to go to the pool without her, and she permitted him to go.

"Did you have anything in mind for tomorrow?" David asked when they were left alone.

"I want to take Gerald to visit Julia. He'll get to meet the baby properly," she answered.

"Do you want company?"

"Yeah, you can come. I'm sure Julia is dying to properly meet you. She's curious about the first guy I've dated in five years."

"I hope she doesn't get overwhelmed by my awesomeness."

She punched his bicep playfully. "You're so full of yourself. She likes you already."

"Her opinion of me matters only as far as it affects what you think of me," he said, getting serious.

She went to the couch he was sitting on and sat next to him. She caught his face in her hands and pecked his jaw first, then his lips.

"Good, because I love you, and that won't change unless you do something to change it."

David deepened the kiss and then let her go with a sigh. She stayed on the couch with him and put her legs up on his thighs.

"I left a few things which I need to get soon. I'll go by sometime next week. I can also take the opportunity to properly resign."

He nodded. "About that. My mum knows we're dating and that you're staying with me."

Makena sat up abruptly and groaned. "What? We agreed we wouldn't tell her. Why did you?"

"Things changed. I had to explain why I had been looking for you frantically, and she wanted to know you would be safe. She liked the idea once I assured her that I was very serious about us."

He looked at her intently as if reading the emotions on her face.

"What did you even tell her? I hadn't told you anything at that point." She sighed in frustration.

"I told her Gerald's father had shown up and was why you left."

She wondered whether David might be a mama's boy. He loved his mother, which she admired, but the fact he'd felt it necessary to share something so private with her made her wonder whether she would have to deal with this throughout their relationship.

"No," he said.

She looked at him questioningly.

"I didn't tell her just for the sake of it. She's very protective when it comes to you. I've told you that. And she was glad that you and Gerald would be safe."

"I wish you hadn't told her, because that means Allison knows, as well. The last thing I want is for your family to think of me as some kind of victim."

David started to say something, but she gave him a sharp look that shut him up. She was done talking about it.

"Should I come with you when you go to get your stuff?" he asked after a few minutes.

She shook her head. "No, I can handle it."

She just had to assure Mrs. Mutua she wasn't a liability.

By evening, she had gotten over her anger. It would be wrong to expect him to keep secrets from his family when she wasn't keeping them from hers. She had told her son and her best friend.

The next day in the afternoon, they went to visit Julia. They stopped by the supermarket for some shopping, and Makena bought a shaker toy for the baby. Julia and David got on famously. Then as Julia and Makena chatted, he and Henry had some beers and watched football. Gerald was thrilled to meet the baby. Julia made a joke about him being her big brother. They had supper together and drove home.

Chapter Thirteen

On Wednesday, Makena finally dared to go see David's mother. She took Gerald with her so he could pick what he wanted from the things they had left behind. It helped that the previous day, Mrs. Mutua had called her and requested she come—she had something for her. They took a matatu to Nairobi and another to Thome Estate where Mrs. Mutua lived.

Some more measures had been taken to secure the compound. There were two more cameras on the entrance than before, and the top of the gate had been reinforced. She rang the bell and announced herself. A security guard opened. The usual gateman was now in the company of a G4S security guard. It seemed David had taken the threat to their security seriously.

Mrs. Mutua was waiting for her outside the door. She embraced her and Gerald and led them inside. She insisted they have lunch first before anything else. Then when they were done, they went to the garden to talk.

"Mrs. Mutua, I'm so sorry for leaving the way I did," she started.

"You don't need to apologize. As a mother, your first priority was your son," she said, taking her hand. Makena was touched by the gesture. "I don't suppose you'll be coming back to work for me?"

"No, that's what I wanted to talk to you about. I wanted to tell you in person. I'll be getting another job soon. I just don't think I should be working for you and dating your son. I wanted to tell you about us when I already had another job."

"You were worried about what I would think when I found out?" Makena nodded. "You didn't have to be. I would never think ill of you. I know you."

"Thank you."

"Don't mention it," Mrs. Mutua said and leaned back. "I didn't just call you for that, though. I'll need your help with your replacement. Allison found someone; she's coming in today. I want you to brief her and also to confirm that she's a good hire."

As they waited for the new caregiver to arrive, Makena went to their house to pack up. Mrs. Mutua had told her the new lady wouldn't be living there so there was no pressure to empty the house. However, she packed up as much of their things as she could. Gerald was happy about taking his toys with him this time. She packed up all their clothes in the large suitcases.

When the new lady showed up, she turned out to be a newly graduated nurse so she was exceptional at her job. Makena requested an Uber to take them home. It surprised her how, after less than a week in David's house, she thought of it as home. She hadn't had one in a long time. Before she left, Mrs. Mutua had packed her some groceries and fruits. Then, she'd handed her a letter which had arrived for her the previous day. It was in an envelope with a letterhead for a law firm. She wondered who it could be from. She put it in her handbag.

It was late in the evening when they got home. David had already arrived and was in the kitchen prepping supper. Makena went and hugged him from behind.

"Your mum was wonderful."

"I know."

"And I have been replaced," she added.

"I know that, too."

"Okay, Mr Know-it-all. What are you cooking?" She leaned against the kitchen counter.

"Beans in coconut sauce, and your favourite, vegetable rice. Here, have a taste."

He took a spoon and scooped some beans from the pot then blew on it to cool it. Makena's lips parted. She opened her mouth, and he fed her. It was tasty. She wasn't a big fan of beans, but this was enough to convert her, and she let him know. His face lit up with pride.

"When you're done cooking, can you come to help me get the rest of our things? I left them in the reception area. I better warn you, our invasion of your house is officially complete," she said with a smile.

"I'm glad. I want you to think of it as your house, too. I had a key made for you," he responded.

After they were done eating and Gerald had gone to sleep, Makena pulled out the letter she had received and read it. She let out a gasp and shook her head furiously. David was by her side in seconds asking her what was wrong, but she barely heard him. She handed the letter to him just to get rid of it. She couldn't believe what was happening.

The letter was from a law firm representing Paul. He was demanding sole custody of Gerald. Paul wanted to take her son away from her. He claimed she was a negligent mother whose promiscuous lifestyle was hindering her ability to be a good parent. He also accused her of keeping her away from his son for five years for no reason.

David pulled out his phone and took a screenshot of the letter. He forwarded it to Allison and then called her.

"Allison, I just sent you something on WhatsApp. Makena's ex is coming after her by suing for sole custody. Please go through it and get back to me."

When he hung up, he took her hands

"Hey, it's going to be okay. We're not going to let him do this okay?"

She pulled her hands away and stood up, then started pacing across the room and biting her fingernails.

"How dare he? He ruined my life. He took everything away from me. I barely escaped with my son, and now, he wants to take him away? He thinks I will sit quietly and let it happen?" she said furiously.

"Allison, who is a damn good lawyer, will go through the letter, and—" Before he could finish, his phone rang. He picked up the call and then handed her the phone. "She wants to speak to you."

"Hi, Makena," Allison greeted. "First of all, I'm sorry about all this. Second, is there any reason why your ex would think that he is in the right? Does he have any evidence to show this? I will also need to know why you thought completely severing ties with him was the right thing to do for Gerald."

Makena was quiet for a long time. She didn't know where to start.

"Okay, why don't we do this? Sleep on this and then tomorrow, we can meet at my office," Allison said.

"Okay, thank you. Have a lovely night."

She handed the phone to David who talked to Allison for a bit before hanging up.

"Oh my God, I have to hire a lawyer and go to court."

"It probably won't come to that, and even if it does, anyone can see that you are a good mother."

She continued pacing up and down.

"Since when has the person on the right tipped the scales to anyone's side? He hounded me all over the country for five years, and now, he wants to take away my son. And let's not pretend that he can't. But I won't go quietly. I will do whatever it takes. I will beg my brother for money to pay for a lawyer. I will sell my parents' land and everything in it. I will take my son and run again."

She was still pacing across the sitting room. She turned and looked at David, started to say something, then stopped. She went and sat next to him and lay her head on his shoulder. He took her hand.

Hours later, she lay in bed wide awake. David was holding her, but she was still, like a tightly wound coil ready to snap. It was a long time before restless sleep finally overtook her. After what felt like a few minutes later, she felt someone shaking her gently and calling her name. She opened her eyes and sat up abruptly.

"What happened? What time is it?"

David gave her a strange look, and she realized her nightdress was soaked with sweat.

"You were screaming and thrashing around. What were you dreaming about?"

She had absolutely no idea what the dream was about. She couldn't remember any of it.

"I don't know. I'm okay now. Go back to sleep," she said quietly.

She checked her phone for the time. It was five-thirty a.m., and she had only slept for four hours. She felt clammy and tired, but she knew she wouldn't be sleeping again. She got out of bed and went to the bathroom, where she had a long, warm shower while she thought about what she would say to Allison. She wasn't sure whether it was a good idea to have her boyfriend's sister defend her in a custody case. However, she didn't know any lawyers. So even if Allison didn't represent her, she would have to be the one to recommend an alternative. She had to tell whoever became her lawyer the whole truth.

IT WAS ALMOST MIDDAY by the time Makena got to Allison's office. David had a meeting early in the morning, then he had come back to stay with Gerald while she was away. He would be doing the rest of the work from home.

Nassir & Co. Advocates occupied most of the twelfth floor of a high-end office building in Upper Hill. Once she arrived, the receptionist ushered her to a conference room and offered her a beverage. She requested water. She waited five minutes for Allison to show up.

"Hi, Makena. How are you?" Allison greeted.

She stood up and shook her hand. Allison had a notebook and a pen and was dressed in a grey pantsuit and had a sleek black weave.

"Hi, Allison. Thank you so much for your help."

"It's not a problem. But I reached out to a colleague who has specialized in family law for most of her career. She is an expert in matters like these."

Makena nodded, and Allison waved at someone from the outside. The colleague turned out to be Caitlin, David's ex. Makena was taken aback.

"Hi, dear. I know the last time we met, I was a bit of a B word, but Allison explained your situation, and I want to help. Besides, it's not like David and I were ever that serious. If it doesn't bother you, I really would like to help you."

Makena was hesitant, but she gave a slight nod. She sat across from her while Allison sat next to her.

"First things first, can you tell me exactly what happened between you two, and why you thought that keeping your son away from him was the best thing to do?"

She took a deep breath and then told them in much detail about the abuse she'd suffered at Paul's hands. When she reached the part about him breaking Gerald's hand, Allison gasped. Throughout the ordeal, Caitlin kept a neutral face.

"After I got better, I moved with Gerald, but he found us, and I moved again. He has chased me around this country for five years. He would send me threatening texts. I did what I had to do to protect my son."

"Do you have the texts he sent you backed up somewhere?"

She nodded. "I have changed phones a few times, but I made sure the messages were backed up on my email."

"That's good," Caitlin said. "According to the letter, he says he wants sole custody and claims you are negligent. Do you think he has anything he can use to prove that?"

"I don't know. When I saw him last week, it was the first time I had seen him in five years."

"Don't worry about it. Whatever he thinks he has, I can counter. I know his lawyer, she's a shark. But that shouldn't worry you, either. From this point on, they only reach you through me. I will reach out to her later today to open communication channels for negotiations. What do you want? Joint custody? Child support? What should I bring to the table?" Caitlin asked.

"I want him to leave us alone for good. I don't want any money for him. I want him to relinquish any claims to my son. I won't take anything less than that."

"Makena, that will be a hard sell."

"It's the only thing I want. Let me know if it's impossible so that I can know what to do next," she said sternly.

"Okay, I'll see what I can do. Meanwhile, if Paul is serious about this, he won't attempt to contact you, threaten you, or stalk you because that will undermine his entire case, so at least for now, you don't have to worry about that."

This would've filled her with relief if it hadn't meant he was trying to make himself into the good guy.

After the meeting, Allison took her to lunch near her office. Caitlin had assured her she would get in touch with Paul's lawyer and call her with feedback later.

"I didn't want you to know. I didn't even want David to know," she said.

"I know. I assure you that I won't be discussing what you told us at today's meeting with anyone, even my brother," Allison said. She ordered them lunch and told her Caitlin was the best lawyer she could trust with her case.

Makena believed her. Caitlin had been honest about her chances. She had also asked her to resist the urge to flee, at least until they gave the legal way a legitimate chance.

Allison drove her home but didn't come in because she had to go back to work. For the rest of the afternoon, Makena tried unsuccessfully to distract herself. She was anxious about Caitlin's call. David was in the office, and Gerald was playing outside. She popped in and said hi to David then went to the kitchen. She did the dishes and took some peas from the freezer to defrost for supper. Then, she sat at the lounger on the balcony reading a book. She read the same page over and over again, unable to concentrate enough to go to the next.

David joined her sometime later. He gave her a peck on the lips and sat next to her. She put the book down.

"How did the meeting go?" he asked.

"As well as could have gone, I guess. Allison won't be representing me, though. Caitlin is. She's a family law specialist, so she is better placed."

She watched him to see his reaction. Aside from surprise, he didn't have another reaction to the news.

"It's true. She was top of her KSL class and is quite dedicated to her career. She's about to be the youngest partner at Nassir & Co," he said.

"You sure you're not just saying that because you used to date her? She apologized, by the way, for being a bitch to me on Gianna's birthday."

"We dated casually, and I never felt for her even a fraction of what I feel for you."

Before she could respond, her phone rang. It was Caitlin. She took a deep breath and picked up the call.

"Hello, Caitlin." she greeted.

"Makena, hi," Caitlin said. Makena tried to detect any feelings from Caitlin, but as she had learnt, she was a professional to a T. "So, I called Paul's lawyer. As I anticipated, they won't agree with any of your demands. He is still asking for sole custody and supervised visitation for you. They claim to have evidence to support their claims and say it will be bad for you if you decide to go to court."

She gasped and placed her hand on her throat. "So he expects me to give him my son, just like that?"

"It seems so," Caitlin said calmly. "They aren't even willing to discuss joint custody, either."

"What happens now?"

"Now, you tell me whether you want this to go to court. Take a few days to decide and let me know. I asked their lawyer to grant us a week, and she agreed. We will need to gather all the evidence you have of his abuse, threats, and stalking. If you have witnesses, that will help, too. The more you have, the better. Again, I ask you to resist the urge to run. If you do, this time, the law will not be on your side."

Makena said okay and then hung up.

"What did she say?" David asked.

"We're going to court. I guess I better call my brother about selling our parents' land. I know this will be an expensive process."

"I wish you would let me help you. It would be my pleasure."

"I know, and I'm not being unreasonably proud or anything like that. You've helped more than you know. You asked your sister to help me who then introduced me to your ex who is now apparently my lawyer. Trust me, you have helped." She kissed his hand. He started to protest but then seemed to think better of it. "I'll wait to talk to my brother until I have all the information. Besides, it's not like I'm asking him for money, merely getting access to my money. Don't overthink this."

A FEW DAYS LATER, SHE called Caitlin and arranged another meeting. She printed all the messages and emails Paul had sent her. She had applied for several jobs now so it seemed she was staying put and was waiting to hear back.

When she arrived at the meeting, Caitlin and Allison were waiting in the same boardroom they had used in the last meeting. She handed the envelope with the messages to her, and Caitlin went through them then set them aside.

"Makena, I want you to know that this will not be easy. Paul is a cop and the son of a former high-ranking officer in the military. They will come at you with whatever force they have. But I will defend you with equal measure. I will do everything in my power to ensure they don't take that beautiful boy from you. Aside from this, I'll need your medical records from any time you were hospitalized due to the abuse. I can reach out to the hospital, or you can get me in contact with any doctor that treated you. We need to stack up as many cards as we can on our deck. I will also need a list of eyewitnesses, neighbours, friends, and anyone who saw what Paul did to you. Character witnesses would be great, too, but no one from the Mutua family, though—they will give a glowing account of your personality and parenting skills, but since you're involved with David, it won't be believable. If it becomes necessary, we can put David on the stand to show you are both providing Gerald with a stable home."

Makena was trying to write everything down to make sure she didn't forget anything.

"Okay. My friend kept in touch with one of my doctors for a while. I'll see if she still has her number. I also wanted to know how much this would cost."

"Absolutely nothing. I'm doing this pro-bono. Any cost on your part will be negligible," Caitlin said.

"Why? Because once I move some things around, I can afford to pay. You don't have to do this for free."

She searched Caitlin's face for any sign. She once again surprised her with her ability to completely keep herself emotionless. Her first meeting with her hadn't given her this impression. She didn't fully trust Caitlin had the right motivation for helping her. So far, she had been completely professional, but now, she was offering her free services. It didn't make sense.

"There are no hidden intentions. I just want to help. I think whatever money you intend to use to pay me can be put to better use. You are a mum who wants what is best for her kid, and you have been through enough. If I thought David was footing the bill, trust me, I would have doubled my fee. But I don't think you would let him, no matter how much he wants. And knowing David, I know he wants to help. I volunteer for FI-

DA legal aid so this is nothing I haven't done before. However, I want you to do something small in return."

Makena waited for the bomb to drop. Maybe she would demand she leave David, or at least move out. It couldn't be good.

"I want you to see someone, a psychiatrist. You should have done this a long time ago, but I understand it was impossible under the circumstances. However, now, you have a moment of pause. It's nothing to be embarrassed about—trust me, most of us need therapy. I can give you a few cards, and you'll see which suits you best. This is non-negotiable."

Makena thought about it for a while and then nodded. It didn't hurt to reach out to one.

Julia had suggested she see a therapist when she was recovering from the incident, but she had resisted the idea. At the time, she hadn't been ready. When she had gotten over her reservations, her life had been too flighty to accommodate having a therapist. This time, she was well settled, she could afford it with her savings, and she was ready. She took the cards Caitlin offered.

"Good. Now, the case won't start until maybe early next year, given that we haven't even been served. But it's coming, that is the impression I got from Paul's lawyer. It's why I insist we be prepared. The letter of service will come through me, and I will let you know as soon as it does. Otherwise, go home and try to put this out of your mind. Enjoy the holidays, go to therapy, and do whatever feels good for you. I've got this handled."

Caitlin said it with so much confidence, she almost had Makena convinced.

Chapter Fourteen

Makena reached out to the psychiatrists Caitlin had recommended until she found one who she felt suited her needs. They arranged a session the following week. It was tough for her to open up to a stranger. For the first session, she barely said anything. She mostly talked about her son and how she was looking forward to going back to school.

She went on a few interviews for the jobs she had applied for. She was offered a position as Program Assistant for an NGO whose headquarters was located close to their home. She would be travelling all over Nairobi County for the job a few days a week, but it was manageable.

The job would be starting at the beginning of the year. It was the best-paying one she had ever had and also the one she looked forward to the most. The NGO worked for the betterment of children living in informal settlements. They provided them with clean water, built classes, and initiated school feeding programmes. Her job was to facilitate support for the teams on the ground and support planning for future programs. She met her boss during the interview, and she liked her.

She called David the minute she got the call to let him know she'd gotten the job.

"That's great, I knew you would get it," he said.

"Thank you, you always believe in me."

"We should celebrate, and thank God it's Friday, as they say. We're going out tonight."

Makena was thrilled. After she hung up, she went to her closet to look for something to wear. Gerald recommended she wear a floral white dress she had recently added to her wardrobe. She held her son's opinion in high esteem, so she agreed. She'd had her nails and hair done earlier in the week.

She called the resident babysitter, Lucy, to plan childcare for the evening—at eighteen years old, just out of high school, she was the daughter of a couple who lived in the building. She picked babysitting jobs in the building to earn a little income. She'd babysat when Makena had gone on interviews and during her therapy sessions. She just watched him and fed him when the time came. Gerald resented the idea of having a babysitter, but he got along well with Lucy, and she liked video games so they played together.

When David came home from work, it was just past seven p.m., and she had already cooked for Gerald. She joined him in the bedroom where he was undressing to take a shower. She undressed and then eyed him with a twinkle in her eye filled with suggestion.

"Want to join me?" she asked.

"First of all, I was first, so I should be the one offering. Second, when have I ever said no to you?"

In the shower, she tied up her braids and covered them with a shower cap and joined him. He kissed her deeply, then before she could take it any further, he stepped away from her and grabbed the shower gel.

"Really?" she asked, filled with disappointment.

"Yes, really. We have a reservation, so we shower, get dressed, and go. We have all night."

"That's one," she said. David gave her a puzzled look. "You've said no to me once."

"It's not a no, baby. It's a *we'll do this later* when I have time to slowly take your clothes off and kiss every inch of you until you beg me to stop. It's a promise."

His eyes were heavy with anticipation.

She coupled her dress with navy-blue heels and simple studs on her ears. The dress had a Chinese collar which opened up to reveal a sensuous hint of cleavage. It hugged her ample curves and went down to slightly above her knees. She applied a little powder, wore lip gloss, and tied her braids up in a bun.

David looked at her in appreciation. He was dressed in black jeans and a white polo shirt and a black trench coat. At his suggestion, she wore a navy-blue trench coat to fend off the cold December night. He refused to tell her where they were going but told her she was dressed appropriately.

It turned out they were going to the popular Brazilian restaurant Fogo Gaucho in Westlands. It was a pleasant surprise for Makena. They were led to their table near the window with a vantage view of the live band playing pleasant jazz music. David ordered them a platter with steak, baked potatoes, and coleslaw. He also ordered wine which was brought for them to drink while they waited.

It turned out to be the best steak Makena had ever had. They sipped their wine and listened to the band after their meal. For the first time in weeks, she was completely relaxed. She wasn't thinking about the case or therapy. She was happy to be there with David, celebrating a brand-new job.

"When do you start the job?" he asked.

"In January, after New Year's. Three more weeks, and my days of being a kept woman will be behind me. I'm going to miss it," she answered with a laugh.

"Well, I wouldn't mind keeping you forever," he said and winked at her.

Her body heated up at the insinuation.

"But I know how important this is for you, which is why we're here celebrating," he added.

"I think It's going to be great. From what I know of the role, it's a challenge, and I haven't had one of those in a while career-wise."

She'd had the chance to ask a few questions about the job, and she understood it wasn't going to be a walk in the park like feeding and medicating a friendly lady. She had actually been pleasantly surprised when she had gotten the job due to her limited experience in the field. She must have given a killer interview. David had helped her with her CV, and they had spent hours in the evening practicing for each of the interviews she'd gone to.

"I'm proud of you for doing this, and I'm glad it makes you happy." He reached out and took her hand and kissed it.

The next three weeks would be a flurry of activity. They had to find a school for Gerald. He hadn't been thrilled about transferring again, but he liked the fact they would be staying with David so this washed away the sting. They would be spending the holidays with his mother, who had called to personally extend an invitation. It had been kind of her to do so because it meant they weren't just being dragged along as David's hangers-on.

After they'd paid their bill, they walked back out. There was a chill which made Makena glad she had taken David's advice and worn a coat. He bundled her in his arms and led her to the car. Once they were in, he pulled out of the parking lot and made the drive home.

Since it was well into the night, there was little traffic, and it only took them thirty minutes to get home. As he pulled into the parking lot, she brushed her hand on his thigh, and he let in a deep breath. When he stopped the car, he reached out and kissed her deeply, then he pulled back and opened his door.

She bit her lower lip lightly. He quickly came around to her side and opened her door, took her hand, and pulled her out of the car. He held her waist, and she arched her neck so could kiss her there.

Before he could go any further, the security guard cleared his throat. They had forgotten all about him. They laughed and headed for the elevator. They could barely keep their hands off each other. When they got to the apartment, they found Gerald had already fallen asleep. Lucy was watching TV. They paid her and sent her home. By the time they got to the bedroom and frantically undressed, they were almost undone by the waiting.

THE FOLLOWING MONDAY, Makena got the call she had been dreading from Caitlin. She had been served, and a hearing was scheduled for February the following year. Caitlin assured her there was enough time to get ready. She promised to call her with updates whenever she could and asked Makena for a list of witnesses who could speak for her.

At therapy, she spoke to Dr. Singh about the latest development. Her joy at having a new job had been dampened by the fact she had to go to court to defend her right to be Gerald's mother. She was angry that after everything Paul had done to her, he was going to make her out to be an unfit mother. Dr. Singh listened as she poured out everything, and when she was done, she told her the same thing Caitlin had said—she had to think about what she was fighting for and find strength in that.

As Christmas approached, she, David, and Gerald had a great time shopping. Gerald insisted they get a tree. Over the weekend, he and David decorated it and put up lights around the living room. They decorated the tree in red, green, white, and gold. They each bought numerous presents for Gerald and laughed at the fact they were spoiling him.

Christmas with the two of them had been fun. She would cook chapatis, even though it was just the two of them. She would buy Gerald two presents, one of his choosing and one she chose for him. He always loved both.

They had each asked him what he wanted. David was tentative with Gearld at first, but he talked to him and convinced him that as long as it was a reasonable gift, he would buy it. Gerald wanted a watch he had seen a neighbour's son with and a camera. Aside from that, they also bought him storybooks, a Scrabble junior board game, and some sports shoes he wanted. Makena had found him a good school in the neighbourhood where several of the kids in the building went. She had taken him for the interview, and he'd liked it. He had gotten so used to change, he remained unfazed by it all.

She went shopping for work outfits, which she enjoyed. Her new job was quite casual, especially on the days she was going to go to the field, but there were weekly meetings which required office wear. That evening, she had modelled some of them for David, and he had been delighted in getting her out of each one. Finally, he couldn't take it anymore, and he'd dragged her to bed and made love to her with the entire contents of her shopping trip around them.

On Christmas Eve, they went to the Capital Centre Mall for some last-minute Christmas shopping. Makena bought a cardigan for Mrs. Mutua and a scarf for Allison. They bought some toys for Nathan and Gianna. It turned out David's family was big into gift-giving for Christmas. They had supper at a restaurant in the mall and went home, where they spent a quiet evening and turned in early.

David and Makena woke up early the next day and put some of Gerald's gifts under the tree. They left him one which he could open when they went to David's mum's house. They were delighted by his reaction. He opened the camera first and took several snapshots of them. They had fluffy banana pancakes for breakfast, which David made. At around ten, they piled up in the car and drove to Mrs. Mutua's.

They were the first to arrive. Mrs. Mutua came out of the house when they arrived and hugged each of them. The house had been decorated much like the apartment. The kitchen was a flurry of activity. They had hired a chef for the morning and a stand-in maid since the usual had gone on holiday. They brought out the gifts and put them under the tree. Allison and her husband and kids showed up a little later.

They chatted and caught up on everything. Mrs. Mutua was surprised to hear about the court case and that Caitlin was representing her.

"Maybe she's done chasing after my son," she said.

"Mum," Allison admonished.

"Well, she always comes here for Christmas, and she didn't come this year. Maybe it has sunk in that she can't sneak into David's bedroom anymore," Mrs Mutua, said shrugging.

"She and I were never in love," David interjected. "Can you not talk about my ex on my girlfriend's first Christmas with us?"

"She's spending Christmas with her grandmother. You know what, I'm glad that she and David are done. Maybe you'll now focus on my friendship with her and see that she is a good friend," Allison said.

"If you say so. Anyway, Makena, if there's any way I can help, let me know," Mrs. Mutua said.

Just before lunch was served, Makena excused herself and went to the guest bedroom downstairs where she sat on the bed for a minute. She had been overwhelmed by all the attention and the familial affection. She thought about how the last time she had been at the centre of a Christmas celebration was eleven years before. She and her parents had been preparing for her future.

The door opened, and Allison stepped in.

"Hey, are you okay?" she asked as she joined her on the bed.

"Yeah, I just needed a minute. As I say that, I realize I left my kid and came hiding," she said with a chuckle.

Allison laughed. "Trust me, you're hardly the first mother to do so. Besides, he's fine. He's keeping Nathan and Gianna entertained with tales of his new school. He seems to love it. How are you doing?"

"I'm thrilled I have a new job, and I hate that I'm about to defend my motherhood in court. So, I'm caught between two very conflicting feelings."

"You're amazing, and I'm not just saying this because you make my brother happy. A terrible thing happened to you, and you have been dealing with it for years. And now, even as you prepare for the fight of your life, you have taken on a new challenge to that. If you and David ever get there, I couldn't have asked for a better sister-in-law."

Makena fought the tears at the corner of her eyes. She nodded in gratitude, unable to say anything.

Allison handed her the shopping bag she had come in with. Makena pulled out a shoe box and opened it. It contained a pair of black designer pumps. They were a sensible three inches.

"For your new job, for luck. When I started my first job, Caitlin got me a pair of heels, and I loved them. Figured I could carry the favour forward. David tells me you love this job. I'm thrilled for you."

She pulled Allison into a hug in an uncharacteristic move. "Thank you, they're lovely."

She tried them on, and they fit like a glove. She put them back in the box and laid it on the bed before they joined the rest of the family in the dining room and lunch was served. There were chapatis, beef stew, fried chicken, baked potatoes, and fruits. Afterwards, they had a fruit cake for dessert.

The children and Mrs. Mutua had fruit juice while the other adults had wine in the living room. Everyone opened their Christmas presents. Mrs. Mutua had gotten all the kids several presents. Makena got a pair of earrings from her and a necklace from Allison and her husband. Allison loved the scarf she had gotten her, and Mrs. Mutua was also grateful for the cardigan.

In the afternoon, they all went to the garden, and Mrs. Mutua showed the kids the trampoline she had installed for them. The kids rushed to it, and everyone looked at Makena. David laughed as he reminded her of how she had been a champ the last time she had been on one. She promised to get on later and entertain them.

It was close to ten p.m. by the time they left. Mrs. Mutua made them promise to bring the kids to her house for New Year's Eve. It was more of a favour to them all so that they could be free to make plans for the night, and they were thrilled to accept. When they got home, Gerald went straight to bed, worn out by the activity of the day. Makena and David spent a few more hours in the living room.

They gave each other presents since they hadn't earlier. She'd gotten him silver cufflinks with his initials engraved. She had looked for days and spent a pretty penny on them. But the look on his face was well worth it. He got her a golf Aurora Enkarta watch which she loved.

ON NEW YEAR'S EVE, Allison picked Gerald up. They had packed him a bag and muffins which he helped bake to take to Mrs. Mutua's. Makena and David spent a quiet evening together watching movies. They did a countdown and kissed when the clock struck midnight, then went to the rooftop to watch the fireworks lighting the Nairobi skyline along with a small crowd of their neighbours.

When the excitement died down, they came back to the apartment. They made love into the wee hours of the morning and slept in. The sun had been up for hours by the time they woke up. They ordered in for lunch and lazed around, then went to pick up the kids later in the afternoon and drove Nathan and Gianna home. Allison and her husband invited them for dinner.

Makena was always surprised by the close relationship between David and Allison. They seemed to have each other's back in a way she and Charlie never had. Maybe the closeness in age helped. Allison was thirty-one and David thirty-four. Their three-year gap was closer than the five years between her and Charlie. She hadn't heard from him all Christmas. She was still smarting over the fact he considered her a failure, and her pride prevented her from reaching out. She wondered whether she could get past it.

She was no longer alone, and the people she surrounded herself with were very protective of her. David had proven he was willing to fight for her, and his mother and sister had embraced her as part of their family.

Then there was Julia, her best friend. She had been there for her in ways that would require several lifetimes to repay. Even now, as she took care of her newborn daughter, she was in constant communication, following up on the case. She had provided Caitlin with the contacts she needed, the doctor for medical background and her parents as character witnesses. She had also taken photos of Makena while she'd been in hospital—which Makena hadn't known all those years—and she sent them to Caitlin.

Makena had been reluctant to involve Julia's parents, but they had been glad to help. They had known her since she was a little girl and had been her parents' friends. She finally had a village within reach after all those years.

As she looked at her son, laughing and playing with Allison's kids, already assuming the role of big brother in the group, she smiled, proud of him.

"Nathan loves Gerald, and Gianna thinks he is such a grownup," Allison's husband said with a smile. "He's a nice kid. He's been helping Gianna figure out some game she got for Christmas and didn't know what to do with. He's very patient with her."

"He's great at making friends. I like that for him," Makena said.

"He's obsessed with video games, so I'm certain it's not a chore. We have to drag him from the screen kicking and screaming," David added.

She looked at him, the fatherly pride he exhibited filling her with love for him.

"Well, you overindulge him because you like them, too. I'm outnumbered, and it's not fun," she said with a fake sulk.

"Maybe we should have a girl. Then you won't be outnumbered."

She turned to look at him, panic filling her at the idea of another child. Allison looked at the two of them and changed the subject. She must have realized this was shaky ground.

When they went home and put Gerald to bed, they retired to their room for an early night.

"I'm sorry I put you on the spot earlier," David said when they were in bed.

"It's okay."

He propped his head on his elbow and faced her. "I just want to know that you're open to the idea, not today, but later."

She was silent for a while, trying to sort out her thoughts.

"Yes, later. We can have this conversation, and I will be open to it."

He pulled her into his arms and kissed her deeply.

Chapter Fifteen

School started the day before her job, so she went with Gerald for his first day. David had insisted on coming, as well. Makena was a little reluctant, but she acquiesced, as she tried to involve him in as much of Gerald's life as she could. However, there seemed to still be a line between her relationship with her son and their relationship, even though they had lived together for over a month.

They were taken around the school again and introduced to Gerald's teacher. Makena put David's name down as the secondary emergency contact. When they were satisfied everything was okay, they left. Gerald would be dropped by the bus, and the headmaster confirmed the bus driver only left after the children were safely inside the gate. This was reassuring for Makena whose priority was her son's safety.

David went to work after dropping her off. She spent the day preparing for her first day at her new job. She had received a few emails from the office regarding what to expect and what potentially her first tasks would be. Her first week would be spent in the office and her second in the field. This would serve as her orientation for the job. Her first month would thus have her learning about the various programs her boss was in charge of.

Gerald was dropped in at four p.m. He regaled her with tales of how amazing his day had been. True to form, he had made friends, and he liked the teachers. The school has a skating rink, and he was to carry his skates on Fridays. It was expensive, but well worth it. David had insisted on paying for him since she hadn't started the process of selling her parents' land yet. She couldn't have been able to afford it otherwise.

She cooked supper for them as he did homework after a snack and shower. David arrived just as dusk was setting in. He joined her in the kitchen and gave her a quick kiss before going back to the living room.

They had a quiet supper and an early night. Makena lay in bed for hours trying to sleep but failing at it. David had started snoring softly beside her minutes after kissing her goodnight. She tried to keep the tossing and turning to a minimum so as not to wake him.

"Can't sleep?" he asked, startling her.

"Yeah, did I wake you? I'm sorry."

He pulled her against his body, and she felt him grow hard against the small of her back.

"Don't be. Maybe I can convince you to fall asleep and not go to your first day of work sleepy," he said.

Before she could ask her how, he flipped her and got on top of her. He supported himself with his hands on either side of her head and kissed her passionately. He went lower to her neck, and then his mouth landed on her hardened nipples. As she gave in to the pleasure, she thought this wasn't such a bad way to convince her to sleep, after all.

"I don't know whether this will help me, but A for effort," she said.

He kissed her lips softly.

"Why don't you keep quiet and let me work? This is worth the midnight wake-up."

He dragged himself under the covers and slid her underwear aside, exposing her sex to his probing tongue. She pressed hard on his shoulders, urging him on. He teased her with his tongue and his expert fingers, bringing her to an orgasm that had her biting on the edge of the duvet to stop herself from screaming. Then, after sheathing himself with a condom from the bedside drawer, he plunged into her gently, holding her wrists as he took her slowly, over and over.

Minutes after their mutual orgasm, she felt herself drifting. She heard him leave the bed to dispose of the condom and didn't hear him get back.

SHE WOKE UP PROMPTLY at six feeling well rested. She pulled on the T-shirt she had abandoned and a pair of tights, then padded softly out of the bedroom and to the kitchen. She wanted to have breakfast ready by the time her boys woke up. Gerald had to be up by six-thirty to get ready for school as the bus picked him up at seven. She and David would leave at seven-thirty, and he would drop her off before driving to his office.

She woke Gerald up when she was done making breakfast. Once he was dressed, he sat down to eat. She went to wake up David, but he was already up, just about to get into the shower.

"You should have woken me up the minute you were awake. I could have helped with breakfast," he said after he'd kissed her good morning.

"I kept you up last night, I was just letting you sleep in a little. Want to share a shower?"

"Always," he said, taking the hem of her shirt to help her out of it. He kissed her passionately.

"No time for anything other than a shower. I don't want to be late on my first day at work."

He expressed mock disappointment. When they were done with the shower, she slipped into another T-shirt and tights and went back to the living room. Gerald was finished with breakfast, and it was time to take him downstairs to get on the bus.

"You don't have to come with me, Mum," he grumbled as she handed him his new school bag.

"It's your first day getting picked. I want to meet the bus driver and other parents."

She turned out to be the only parent there. The kids all waited inside the gate, and when the bus arrived, the driver honked, and the security guard let them out. Gerald was embarrassed because he had already met most of the kids. He didn't even hug her goodbye. The driver was a nice lady—she realized how nervous Makena was and assured her her son would be safe.

She felt stupid about being a worry wart, but she was in a whole new territory. She was living in a whole new part of the world and starting what could be her dream job.

"I'm a mother hen," she told David when she joined him for breakfast after dressing for work. For her first day, she'd chosen a navy-blue pencil skirt, a pink silk blouse, and a striped navy-blue blazer. She coupled the look with the pumps she got from Allison.

"And a very sexy one, at that. You look gorgeous," David said, giving her a once-over. "You're starting your first day of work, and there have been a lot of changes in your life this past couple of months. Gerald is the one constant in all of it. It's okay to be a mother hen with him."

"You're good at handling me," she said, then turned to him with a serious look. "I'm not the only one who has had a lot of change thrust his way. One minute, your apartment is a bachelor pad, and the next, it's a full-on family apartment with a little boy's room. Are you okay with that? It was a bit fast, and I would understand if you were feeling some type of way about it."

He took her hand and kissed the back of it.

"I'm perfectly fine with it. You and Gerald made my house a home, and I wouldn't have it any other way."

As he drove them to work, she thought about what he had said. He had made her feel secure in the new normal they were navigating. He knew just how to reduce her fears.

He stopped the car outside the gates of the building she would be working from—a small office complex along Mombasa Road not far from his own offices. He gave her a quick peck on the lips and wished her luck on her first day.

"Call me during your lunch break to let me know how it's going."

She nodded and got out of the car, waved him off, and took a deep breath and walked inside. She introduced herself to the security guard and was let through. The receptionist directed her to her supervisor's office.

"Good morning, Makena. Welcome," she greeted as soon as Makena walked in, then directed her to one of the seats in front of her desk.

"Thank you. I'm happy to be here," Makena said enthusiastically.

Her supervisor, Mrs. Otieno, was an older woman probably in her mid-forties.

"Great. Here are some files on the projects we are working on for you to orient yourself with. Don't worry, I don't expect you to get through them all today. Do as much as you can, and if you have questions, I will assign you a peer to help you out. You need to have the information down for when you go into the field next week."

She handed Makena several files. When they were done, Mrs. Otieno took her to her cubicle. It contained a desktop, a notebook, pens, and a calendar inscribed with the NGO's green and white logo.

Makena's first day was just a lot of reading. The files contained the projects, budgets, specifics, and the staff involved. She read and took notes. She met the colleague Mrs. Otieno had mentioned. Betsy had been in the NGO for two years. She was also a program assistant but was on the fast track for a promotion. The first step was taking Makena under her wing. She had the cubicle next to hers.

"Time for lunch, Makena. I'll show you a place," Betsy said as one p.m. rolled in.

Makena was relieved to have a break from the files. She put them in the drawer and locked it then grabbed her purse and followed Betsy. The place was a restaurant in the next building.

Betsy swore they had the tastiest food around and they were affordable.

They had rice, beef stew, and steamed cabbage.

"How are you liking your new job?" Betsy asked her.

"It's great, very different from what I did before," she answered.

"What did you do before?"

"I was a home caregiver. I wanted something different, and I got it."

Betsy talked her ear off about the projects she had worked on and what to expect in the coming days. Makena appreciated it because she wasn't that much of a talker.

As they walked back to the office, Betsy reiterated her offer to help her in any way, insisting it was part of her job. Before they walked in, Makena excused herself to call David. He picked up on the first ring.

"Hello, gorgeous. How are you?"

She sighed at the sound of his voice. "It's great so far. I love it. I've mostly spent the day reading up on projects, but they're essential."

"That's great. I'm glad you're loving it. Did you have lunch?"

"Stop babying me. Of course I had lunch."

He laughed. "Okay, I'll back off, see you at home."

She blew him a kiss and hung up. She was still getting used to being taken care of. David was meticulous about it, and she worried he might feel like she was just someone for him to take care of rather than a partner. She had needed him and leaned on him, but he had never needed her for anything. She shook those thoughts away as she glanced at her watch—her lunch break was over.

The rest of her first week went by without a hitch. By the time she was done with the files, she could answer any question on the projects she had been assigned. Betsy quizzed her to ensure she was ready for the next part of her orientation. She was also acquainted with the organization's vision and mission statements.

Her second week at work was extremely different. After a quiet weekend at home, she was back to work on Monday. David dropped her off at the office, and she was immediately picked up by one of the company's vans. Betsy had advised her to dress casually for the day. She was given a black shirt with the company's logo, and she coupled it with blue jeans and sneakers. Betsy, who was going with her, was dressed the same.

"How was your weekend?" Betsy asked as the van cruised to Lang'ata Road.

"It was quiet. I was just home with my kid and boyfriend," Makena answered, realizing she had just dispensed some unnecessary personal information to Betsy.

"You have a kid?" Betsy asked, surprised.

"Yeah, a nine-year-old son," she said, her face lighting up. She pulled out her phone and showed Betsy a photo of Gerald from Christmas. Betsy remarked about what a handsome little boy he was before handing her back the phone.

"How was your weekend?" Makena asked her.

"It was great, though I may have overindulged on Saturday. I went out with some friends, and I can still feel it in my head," Betsy said, rubbing her forehead gently.

"Sorry," she sympathized.

The van stopped on the outskirts of Kibera. There was a small building painted white and green with the organization's name and logo on the side.

"This is one of our field offices. It mostly deals with adult literacy and income-generating projects for women," Betsy said as soon as they alighted from the van. She handed her one of the files Makena had been studying the previous week.

In the course of the week, she met several people who had benefited from the organization's programs and those who were currently in them. She got involved in the work, participating in a different area every day. The organization also collaborated with others and provided resources which she and Betsy were overseeing for the week.

She had been so engaged with work, the case took a backseat in her mind. It wasn't until therapy when Dr. Singh asked how she was handling all the activities in her life after the extended period of quiet that she thought about it. Over the weekend, she had seen Julia who'd told her Caitlin had been in touch and she had given her everything she had, including the doctor's contacts and some photos she took of her while Makena was in the hospital. She was also willing to testify for her.

Over the past few weeks, she hadn't heard much from Caitlin except to assure her everything was going on well. The case was scheduled to start in about a month.

JUST LIKE THAT, HER month-long probation period was over. Betsy gave her a glowing review, and she returned the favour. She was finally integrated into a team. They were all lovely people, and she realized she was really doing her dream job. At home, she couldn't be happier. She was getting constant updates from Gerald's teachers as to how he was a stellar student. He seemed to adjust well, just like he had his entire life.

The idea of domestic bliss had always been foreign to her. She couldn't imagine, after Paul, that she would find a relationship in which she was completely happy. And yet, she got it with David. She loved him fiercely. Other than her son, he was the most important person in her life. She couldn't imagine how she'd almost walked away from him because of Paul. Paul had taken away almost everything from her, and he almost took away the best thing to have happened to her since she'd left him.

She would come home from work and find David and Gerald waiting for her, happy to see her. Gerald would offer a fist bump, and David would kiss her. If he got home before her, he would prepare Gerald a snack and help him with homework. She was happy to let him do this because he was better at it. When she got home, she would cook, and they would sit together in front of the TV and talk about the day they'd each had. Gerald had joined the debate team at school and played in the skating and swim teams. David was working on the company's finances and had discovered they were struggling a little, so they were holding off on any further expansions. It was weighing on him, but he appreciated having someone to talk about it with.

As the case loomed around the corner, it came to the forefront of her mind. She talked to her boss who agreed to give her the week of the case off, telling her nothing was more important than family. Caitlin had told her the testimonies would take a few days so she wouldn't need too much time off. She had decided to testify after Caitlin let her know hers was the most important testimony.

Her witnesses included Julia, the doctor, and Gerald's teacher from his former school. Caitlin had gotten a list of Paul's witnesses including a neighbour, the cop he had been cheating on her with, and Ricky. She was shocked to see Ricky on the list, because he didn't know anything about her life, unless he was planning to lie.

Chapter Sixteen

The first day of the trial was a Monday. While Caitlin had told her she didn't have to be there, she couldn't stomach the thought of not knowing what was going on. So she decided she had to go. Paul's lawyer and his witnesses would go first. Caitlin had said he wasn't on the witness list at first but he might be added later, so it was better for her to be prepared for the eventuality.

On the first day of the trial, she wore a purple dress with a white collar. She didn't wear any jewellery aside from her watch. Caitlin had advised her that the spotlight wouldn't be on her as it would be when she testified. All she had to do was sit and listen and limit her reactions as much as she could.

"I should come with you," David said as they had breakfast.

"No, you have a lot to do at work, and Caitlin said today won't be that hard. All I have to do is just sit there. Don't worry, Allison will be there, and I'll call you if I need you," she reassured him.

He made her promise to call if she needed him then kissed her goodbye and left for work.

Makena took a cab to the court. The case was being heard at Milimani Law Courts children's court. Caitlin was already there with Allison. Allison hugged her, and they walked to the courtroom.

Paul arrived a few minutes later, hand in hand with his mistress, who it now seemed was his pregnant wife. He eyed Makena, and she felt a chill down her spine. Her heart beat rapidly, and she gripped her wrist so hard, her nails broke her skin. She wished she had let David come with her. She felt Allison grip her shoulder reassuringly from behind her. Paul's parents also showed up. Just before the judge arrived, Julia walked in and sat next to Allison. Although she had reassured her she didn't have to come, seeing her caused relief to wash over her.

The judge asked whether they were sure they wanted to go through the trial, reiterating that they could go through mediation instead. Caitlin looked at Makena, and she nodded. Paul's lawyer also agreed to the case going forward.

They were each given a chance to give opening statements. Paul's lawyer declared her intention to prove to the courts that Makena was an unfit mother and that her behaviour had led to Gerald's instability. She mentioned the moving around and the cutting of contact with Paul, and called any accusations she may have against Paul false.

Caitlin stood up to give her opening statements. She detailed the abuse Makena had suffered at Paul's hands and Gerald's injury. She also talked about the threats and how Makena had done what was necessary to protect her son. She reiterated she had witnesses and evidence to show this.

Paul's lawyer was the first to call his witnesses. Makena and Caitlin had gone through the list, and she was sure there was nothing to be alarmed about. Paul's wife, Rachel, was called first. After her introduction, the lawyer proceeded to question her.

"Before you were Paul's wife, you were his friend and colleague, right?" the lawyer asked.

Rachel nodded, and the lawyer told her she had to say it out loud.

"Did you ever witness any interactions between Paul and his son, Gerald?"

"Yes, Paul is a good father, and he loves his son dearly. He played with him and was the disciplinarian. Beyond that, he was the financial provider. He fed him, clothed him, and paid his school fees. Gerald's mother didn't have a job. She stayed home all day waiting for Paul to provide everything, which he did dutifully. She was unstable and would often make up stories about Paul to tarnish his name, but Paul always forgave her because he is a good father and wanted what was best for his son," Rachel said.

Makena gasped loudly, and Caitlin shot her a warning look.

"When Makena left with Gerald and didn't communicate with Paul, how was that for him?"

"It was terrible. As I said, Paul loved his son, and he knew that Makena was disturbed, so to have her be Gerald's sole caregiver was hard. Paul tried everything. He would look for them, and when he found them and tried to get Makena to at least let him see his son, she would disappear. She moved the boy all over the country for years rather than let him see his father. I can't imagine how terrible it must have been for Gerald."

"You're Gerald's stepmother, so if Paul is successful and is granted sole custody of Gerald, you will be one of his guardians. How do you feel about helping raise a child who isn't yours?"

"Gerald is my husband's son. For that reason, he will be just like mine. I will treat him the same as I will treat his soon-to-be-born sibling. We have had a room ready for him in our house for years. I will love him, protect him, and care for him just like any mother would, like his own mother has failed to do."

Rachel looked at Makena, and on seeing the horrified look on her face, she smiled, a smile so tiny that if Makena hadn't been looking at her, she would have missed it.

"Is Paul a good father?"

"Yes. I wouldn't be married to him and expecting his baby if he wasn't." She smiled and gently caressed her belly.

The lawyer was done, and it was Caitlin's turn. She stood up and walked over to Rachel.

"Congratulations on your marriage and pregnancy." Rachel nodded. "How long have you and Paul been together?"

"We got married two years ago."

Two years ago, Makena had been living in Nyeri, and Paul had found them. The threats he'd included in his texts had been so horrifying, she'd left immediately.

"How long were you together before that?" Caitlin asked.

Rachel shifted uncomfortably. "We were friends for years and got together after Makena left."

"Isn't it true that your relationship was one of the factors that led to the breakdown of his marriage to Makena?"

Paul's lawyer stood up quickly. "Objection! Where is this heading to? It's Paul's relationship with his son we're here to talk about."

"Your honour, it is important to establish what the relationship between the two was before the breakdown of the marriage which led to the estrangement between Paul and his son," Caitlin explained.

The judge nodded and overruled the objection.

"Makena and Paul weren't legally married," Rachel said.

Caitlin chuckled. "They had lived together for five years and were raising a son. Did he tell you they were just roommates?"

"Uh...no," Rachel answered nervously.

"To the best of your knowledge, what led to the breakdown of their relationship, and why did Makena feel the need to cut Paul out of their son's life?"

"Makena got up and disappeared with the boy when Paul told her he wanted to break up with her. He offered to help her financially and pay child support. He wanted them to co-parent, but she took Gerald and left to punish him knowing how much Paul loved his son."

"You said you were one of his colleagues, right?" Rachel nodded. "Did you know about Paul's violent streak when you married him? More importantly, did you know that he had been accused of physical abuse by Makena several times?"

"Paul was never abusive to Makena. She started those rumours to tarnish his good name."

Caitlin walked back to their table and took a photograph and a document which she handed to Rachel.

"Could you please tell the court what the document in your hand is?"

"It's a filled P3 form," Rachel answered after barely glancing at the paper.

"Whose name is indicated as the Officer Commanding Station?"

Rachel was silent for several seconds, glancing nervously at Paul. Then, at the judge's prompting, she responded that the signature was hers.

Caitlin asked her to list the injuries confirmed by the doctor on the form.

There was a black eye, a busted lip, and a sprained wrist.

"Did you see the injuries yourself? It is standard procedure to do so before signing a P3 form," Caitlin asked.

"Yes... Yes, I did see them. But there's no guarantee that Paul caused them. They could have come from anyone," Rachel continued.

Caitlin cut her short, and the judge dismissed her. As she went to sit down, Paul stood up and held out his hand to her. Then he hugged her, looking straight into Makena's eyes.

Makena felt a pang of something she did not want to dwell on.

The next witness was a neighbour from the time she and Paul lived together. As the examination progressed, Makena realized she was the person Gerald had run to during the final attack and who had helped get her to hospital.

However, she testified for Paul and tried to paint her as irresponsible. She blamed Gerald's injury on her and said her injuries were from a fall. Makena had never had a close relationship with her neighbours because she was embarrassed that they knew about her issues with Paul. But it pained her to see someone who had seen her beating first-hand lie with a straight face.

"She's the one who found me, but I don't remember any of it," she whispered to Caitlin.

When Paul's lawyer was done examining the neighbour, Caitlin asked for a short recess. They were given an hour, during which they went for lunch in a cafe near the court.

"Well, that was bad. How well did that woman know you?" Caitlin asked.

Makena thought back to when she was her neighbour. They had barely interacted. Her daughter and Gerald went to the same nursery school, but there was nothing beyond that. She barely even talked to her. She wouldn't have even remembered her name. She didn't leave the house a lot when she lived with Paul. It had been a lonely existence that alienated her from everyone she could have gone to for help, and she told Caitlin as much.

"Do you think she's being vindictive?" Caitlin asked.

"No. Ricky will probably be, but this lady, she's nice. When my son went to her, she made sure I got to a hospital. Maybe Paul has something on her or maybe he's threatening her."

"Either way, she's going to tell the truth. I'll make sure of it. At least, we know what to expect with Ricky. I'm sure he will be a man scorned, and I know how to deal with those. If that poor woman is being threatened, then I'm sorry for what's about to happen to her," Caitlin said.

Makena closed her eyes for a second, knowing nothing would compare to knowing Paul would never bother her again. She was going to do whatever it took to make that happen.

"Do whatever you have to do," she said.

When they returned to court, Caitlin was called to question the neighbour.

"You said that Makena was an irresponsible mother. Can you elaborate on that?" she asked.

"Gerald usually didn't have supervision. She would let him play outside and not come to check in on him for hours. He also missed meals and was very thin for a child his age. My daughter who is the same age must have had easily three kilograms over Gerald. I would often feed him. Also, when she was fighting with her husband, she let him get hurt in the process."

"Are you a doctor, or a nurse?" Caitlin asked, and the woman shook her head. "Let the record show that the witness is not a doctor and is not qualified to comment on the health of the child. Now, let's talk about this fight. What did you witness on the night in question?"

"I heard noises coming from their house, but it's something we were used to, so we didn't interfere. Then Gerald came banging at our door, crying. When I opened the door, he was holding onto his arm. I let him in and asked him what was happening."

"Do you remember exactly what Gerald told you?" The lady looked first at Makena, then at Paul, and she saw a look of fear pass over her face. "Please answer the question."

"He said 'Please come, Daddy is hurting Mummy,'" the woman said.

"When you went to their house, what did you see?"

This time, the woman didn't hesitate. Makena noticed a shift in her demeanour. She was not skirting around questions or giving rehearsed answers.

"The first thing I saw was the glass coffee table. It was broken to pieces. Makena was lying next to the TV stand, curled into a ball. Paul was nowhere to be seen. I tried to talk to her, but she was unconscious. She was injured badly, and there was blood everywhere. I called my husband, and we took her to the hospital. We made sure she was checked in and gave them her husband's number. Since we had her phone, I called her friend who I put in contact with the hospital since Paul wasn't picking up his phone."

"Did you ever hear from or see Makena and Gerald again?" Caitlin asked.

"No, we went back to the hospital the next day and found that they had been transferred to Kijabe," she answered.

"How long did it take Paul to realize that his wife and son were gone? Please answer to the best of your knowledge."

"Paul came back two days later. He knocked on our door and asked whether we knew where Makena had gone because his house was a mess. I told him we took her to the hospital. He didn't ask after the boy or ask what hospital we took them to."

Caitlin dismissed her.

So far, Paul's witnesses had fallen apart on him. The last was Ricky, and they were optimistic about him, too. When he was called to the stand, he painted a picture of Makena as the seductress single mother who was out to ensnare the dads in her son's school. He accused her of coming on to him and soliciting money. He also said that her son had behavioural issues and had gotten into fights.

Caitlin dug into the angle of him being a man scorned. He was the one who called Paul, and she asked why he did that.

"A boy needs his father, especially one with a mother as neglectful and irresponsible as Makena. She is more concerned about money and getting the next man than she is about her child."

"Did you know why they had separated?"

"No, but I asked Paul, and he said Makena had just taken the boy and disappeared, which is wrong."

"Why did you take it upon yourself to find him? Isn't it true that you harassed this woman for months and brought her abusive ex-husband back into her life as an act of revenge for her rejection?"

"I wasn't interested in her. She's a cold bitch who thinks herself too good for the rest of us," Ricky said.

There was a gasp from someone in the crowd, but Makena schooled her face to look neutral. Caitlin allowed Ricky's outburst to soak in before letting him go. The court was dismissed for the day.

When Makena got home, the first thing she did was hug Gerald. He looked at her curiously when she released her.

"Are you okay, Mum?"

"Yeah, I just missed you."

She strode to the bedroom, and David followed her. She set her purse down and started undressing for a shower. He pulled her into a hug, and she sniffled.

"How was it?"

She dropped heavily on the bed, in her underwear.

"Hard. It's crazy. I listened to people who hardly know me telling lies about me, and now, I get to listen to the people who do know me tomorrow and hope it will be enough to prove I can keep my son. I cannot imagine it going badly. He is my whole life." She leaned her head on his shoulder.

"If you need me to testify, or just be there, all you have to do is tell me. Don't shut me out of this. I love him, too."

"I know." She gave him a brief kiss. "It means a lot to me that you love him. But I don't want you to come to court, and if it becomes necessary for you to testify, I will let you know. Allison and Caitlin are with me, and I'm okay."

"I'll finish up with Gerald's homework," he said and stalked out.

Makena had a feeling she had upset him somehow. Even later that night, when they were in bed and he turned away from her, she couldn't bring herself to reach out and ask why. Her plate was filled to the brim, and whatever was stewing with David, she would deal with it later, once she knew her son was safe with her forever. So she turned to her side and closed her eyes.

MAKENA'S FIRST WITNESS was Dr. Shikuku who had been her doctor at Kijabe. She explained all her injuries using the X-ray images and photos Julia had taken of her. She also talked about treating Gerald's wrist and her conversation with him where Gerald said his father had pushed him and hurt his mum. She stated the injuries were consistent with a beating.

When Paul's lawyer asked why she had treated her and not reported to the police, she said the case had been an emergency. The lawyer asked her what Makena said caused the injuries once she was able to speak. Makena remembered telling the doctor she'd had a bad fall. She thought about what a cliche it was.

Next came Gerald's teacher from the school he went to while they lived with Mrs. Mutua. Her testimony blew Ricky's lies away. She talked about how great of a student Gerald was. He had excellent grades and was well-liked by the teachers and his classmates. She said Makena had shown up for all meetings and on the school sports day cheering Gerald on.

"In your opinion, is Gerald a well-adjusted child?" Caitlin asked.

"Yes, he is," the teacher said.

Paul's lawyer asked her about the day Paul showed up. But when she responded that Gerald's reaction had been fear, she didn't ask her any more questions.

Julia was called to the stand after a lunch recess.

"Julia, how well do you know Makena?" Caitlin asked.

Julia looked at Makena and gave her a warm smile. She smiled back.

"Extremely well. We have been friends for close to twenty-five years, and I'm Gerald's aunt," she answered.

"Seems like you're close. And how well do you know Paul?"

"I don't know him all that well. I know him as my best friend's ex, the man who beat her up several times and used his authority as a police officer to cover it up."

Paul's lawyer objected to the last statement.

Caitlin followed up by asking about Makena's relationship with her son, especially when they were no longer living with Paul.

"The first days were hard after she left the hospital. They were staying with us because she knew that she needed help. Aside from the physical part, she was dealing with the end of her relationship. She was worried about her son and what it would do to him that his father had hurt him. It didn't take her long to get out of the depression and do what needed to be done for her son. She found a job and a safe place for them to live."

Paul's lawyer asked her whether she had ever heard of Paul hurting Gerald before, and she responded no.

Julia's testimony was the last of the day, and Makena would testify the next day. Caitlin mentioned she wanted to ask Paul to testify since his own lawyer wasn't. Caitlin drove her back to her office to prepare her for her testimony.

When she went home, she resisted the urge to pull Gerald into a hug again because it would have weirded him out. Instead, she sat with him and helped him with his homework. Then, she asked him to help her in the kitchen. He liked grating carrots because he got to eat the tips. So she gave them to him and set him up on a stool.

"How do you like your new school?" she asked.

"It's great. I made a friend. He likes video games, too. Maybe later he can come to visit?" She nodded. "I started playing the violin during music class. I'm not good yet, but the music teacher said if I practise, I can get better. Math is harder, but Uncle David is helping me get better. He's good at math."

"I'm an accountant, I have to be good at math," David said as he stalked into the kitchen.

When Makena came home, he had been in the office, and she hadn't wanted to bother him. She knew deep down they were icing each other, but she didn't know what was bothering him.

"Hi," she greeted.

He kissed her cheek.

When they were done eating supper, Gerald went to bed. Makena and David stayed up a while longer.

"How was court today?" he asked.

"It was good. Julia testified, and the doctor at the hospital, and Gerald's former teacher. I think we're good so far," she said with a smile. Caitlin had told her to be cautiously optimistic.

"Allison told me you will testify tomorrow. Do you want me to come?"

He was extending an olive branch, and yet, she couldn't bring herself to take it. They were going to cut her open and let all the junk fall out. She wouldn't let him hear it. All the terrible things Paul had done to her, her fears, and all her pain would be examined to the last detail. Caitlin had spent hours preparing her for it. She wouldn't let him see that. So she deflected.

"Why are you talking to Allison about this?" she asked, scooting away from him on the couch they were sharing.

"Because you won't talk to me, and I don't want to push. I know this is hard for you."

"I've just spent hours preparing for tomorrow, I will be fine," she said. Then she told him goodnight and went to bed, knowing she was pushing him away.

Chapter Seventeen

On the last day of the trial, Makena overslept. David shook her gently to wake her up. She sat up with a start and checked the time—it was six-thirty a.m., the time she woke Gerald up after preparing breakfast. She scrambled to catch up. She woke him up and went to the kitchen, prepared just enough tea for him to save time, and spread three slices of bread with Blueband and jam. When he was done and off to school, she made them breakfast and went to take a shower. She wore a maroon blouse and a black pencil skirt and black pumps.

David insisted on driving her to court. Caitlin and Allison were already there, and Julia called to say she was on her way. David kissed her, and they walked in. They were a few minutes early.

"Are you ready?" Caitlin asked.

"I'm ready," she answered.

She felt well prepared for this. Surprisingly, she had slept through the night and hadn't woken up once. The nightmares she had grown accustomed to in stressful situations didn't come, either. She had a good morning, having shelved whatever was happening between her and David. He had been great, encouraging her. He had held her in the car until she was ready to get out of it. He'd also asked if she wanted him in court, but she'd said no.

Paul came alone—he didn't bring his wife or parents. His side of the court was empty. When their eyes met, he shot her a look that caused her to tremble, and she quickly looked away.

When the judge arrived, Makena was called up. She sat on the witness docket and was handed a bible. She placed her hand and swore to tell the truth.

Caitlin stood up to question her. She walked up to her and whispered, "This will be over soon."

Makena nodded. When she looked up, her eyes met David's, and he smiled at her. Although she had told him numerous times not to come, seeing him there meant more than she could ever imagine.

"Makena, tell the court about your relationship with Gerald's father."

She took a deep breath and started.

"I met Paul when I was nineteen years old, and we started dating. Soon after, I got pregnant. He didn't take it well. He said that I had done it to trap him, so we broke up. Eventually, he came around and sought me out. I was reluctant to get back together with him because the breakup had been ugly, and that was when I started to discover he has a temper. But I wanted my son to have a family, a mum and dad, and I was scared I couldn't raise him by myself. My parents had died just a few months earlier. So Paul and I moved in together. I was still in college and kept that up with a lot of resistance from him. He wanted me to drop out."

"When you had your son, how did you feel about being a mother?" Caitlin asked.

"The day I had Gerald, Paul was away. I went into labour, and he wouldn't pick up the phone. My friend Julia was with me, and it took twenty hours of labour for Gerald to be born. They handed me my son, and the first time I saw him, it was like looking at the sun," she said, a smile lighting up her face.

"I knew very little about how to be a mum. I was twenty and had never even changed a diaper, and I was terrified to bathe him because he was so little. He had terrible colic and kept me up for hours. But every day, I got better at being his mum. I promised him that I would never let anyone hurt him, and my greatest regret is that I couldn't keep that promise."

She paused for a moment.

"I was alone a lot when he was a baby. He would cry all night long, and that irritated Paul, so he would go away for several days, show up, and do it all over again. Since I didn't have a job, I relied on him for everything, and even after Gerald was born, when it wasn't just me, he would still go for days and leave us with nothing to eat. The first time he hit me, it was because I asked where he went as he was headed out and I asked him to leave us some money for food. He told me it was none of my business and slapped me. I wanted to leave immediately."

She stopped, then looked at Paul, and he had the look he always had that caused her to recoil into herself.

"Take your time," Caitlin said.

Paul's lawyer started to object, and Paul held her back. Caitlin looked at them curiously.

"He was remorseful, or so I thought. He opened a bank account for me which he would fund monthly, and for a while, things were great. Then I found out about the cheating, and when I confronted him, he beat me. This time, it wasn't just a slap. He banged me up so bad that I needed to go to the hospital. That is when I had the P3 filled by Rachel. At the time,

I didn't know she was the one he was cheating with. I took my son and left. I went to my parents' house in the village. A few weeks later, he tracked me down. This time, I was more resistant, but he wooed me. He begged and cajoled. He came every day and promised it would never happen again.

"He proposed to me over this grand dinner he took me to. After that, I lost count of how many times he laid a hand on me and for what reason. Then I got pregnant again. I was terrified to tell him. When I did, he was happy about it, and things were calm. That is, until I found out that he was unfaithful, again. When I confronted him, this time, he didn't stop."

She had to stop here to inhale sharply.

"It was like he was possessed. He punched me and kicked me everywhere. I was three months pregnant, so my first thought was the baby. I curled into a ball so the baby wouldn't get hurt. He threw me around, and I got hit on the furniture. Gerald had been in the bedroom the whole time. He knew not to come out when his daddy and I were fighting. The noise from all the knocking furniture must have worried him because he came running. He stood between Paul and me to try and stop him from hitting me. Gerald, my four-year-old son, stood up to Paul, and for his trouble, Paul pushed him. That's how he broke his wrist. At some point, I lost consciousness. When I came to, I was in the hospital."

She stopped talking as the tears started welling up in her eyes, and she pulled out a tissue from her purse.

"What happened in the hospital?" Caitlin asked.

Makena took a deep breath and closed her eyes, then she opened them. Everyone was looking attentively. The judge was taking notes.

"My jaw was wired shut for six weeks because he broke it, so for six weeks, I couldn't talk. I had a cast on my left hand all the way to the shoulder. There were bandages on my ribs, and I had several cuts and bruises which were stitched up. For some of them, I still have scars. But all that was nothing compared to finding out that my baby was gone. The physical trauma caused me to have a miscarriage." She sniffled and wiped her tears.

"At which point did you decide that both you and Gerald would be better off without Paul?" Caitlin asked.

"It wasn't something I spent a lot of time contemplating. The minute I regained consciousness, I decided that I was never going back to him. When I recovered, I looked for a job in a different town. I didn't want to make it easier for him to find us. But he did, and he texted a photo outside Gerald's school gate to prove it. I was terrified, so we moved. Whenever I went, we would stay a few months, and he would find us. His texts soon became threatening. He would text me emojis of guns and a blown head. This scared me because when we would argue, back when we were still together, he would place the gun on the table, just to show me that it was within reach if he wanted to use it. So I kept running."

"Have you ever neglected your son?" Caitlin asked.

"Never," Makena answered forcefully. "Even when I was in the hospital, I knew he was safe. I know where he is at all times, even when he is not with me. I have never intentionally hurt him. But I know that staying with Paul was hurting long before his arm broke. He was scared all the time, he was isolated because most of the kids didn't want to play with him, and he didn't, either. Staying with Paul would have destroyed him.

I don't regret leaving or keeping my son away from that monster," she declared forcefully.

When she looked up, Paul was looking at her smugly, and David was gone. She didn't know exactly when he had left. Caitlin was done questioning her, and Paul's lawyer didn't have any questions, so she was dismissed. It was almost lunchtime, and the judge asked for a recess. Caitlin told her she would call Paul to the stand as a hostile witness.

"Where do you want to go for lunch?" Julia asked.

Makena shook her head. "I think I'll just head home for a bit."

She called David, and he didn't pick up. She was about to request an Uber when Julia offered to drive her.

"I think you're going to win. I was looking at the judge, and there's no way he is going to let Paul have Gerald after everything you said. Plus I thought Paul's lawyer was good, but she didn't offer a lot of resistance to your testimony."

"I wondered about that, too. At some point, she wanted to object, but Paul stopped her. She looked pretty upset about it. Or maybe he was so unbothered because they already have the judge in their pocket. His parents are rich. If it came down to bribing, it wouldn't be an issue for them."

"You can't think like that. You are on the right side of this. If it doesn't go your way, we will raise hell on him. We won't let him get away with what he did to you. From what Caitlin says, you can even sue him for abuse with all the evidence you have gathered. At the very least, he will lose his job, and there will be a review of his behaviour."

Makena nodded.

"I think David is upset with me. I didn't want him to come to court, but he did anyway, and then he left even before my testimony was over," she said, her voice softened with concern.

"I did wonder why he wasn't in court. Why would you ask him not to come?"

"He doesn't know the extent of his abuse, and I wanted to keep it that way. I never want him to see me as a victim."

Julia pulled up outside the apartment.

"Do you want to come in?"

"No, I think you and David need to talk. Call me later."

She gave her a hug, and Makena got out of the car. David's car was in his parking space in the lot, which meant he was home. She got on the elevator and pressed the button to their floor. Her feet were jelly as she walked to the door. She contemplated turning around, refusing to believe that while fighting for her son, she was gearing up to pick a fight with her boyfriend. As if there wasn't enough turmoil in her mind. She shook her head and inserted her key into the lock.

As she walked in, she heard David's voice. He was in the kitchen talking on the phone. At first, it was muffled, but it rose quickly.

"How could you not have known? Her life was in danger. That man almost killed her, and she spent years running for her life. You're her brother, you were supposed to protect her."

Makena dropped her bag and rushed to the kitchen as she realized he was talking to Charlie.

"Hang up the phone," she ordered.

He shook his head and downed whatever amber-coloured liquid he had in his glass.

"You should have known because you should have checked up on her. When she was in hospital for six weeks and couldn't speak, you should have asked why. When she kept moving all over, you should have wondered why she was doing that. But you never did, and now, she could lose her son, and you still have no idea."

She tried to reach for the phone from him, but he swung away.

"Please stop talking," she begged.

"Why is it my business? Because I love her!" He hung up the phone and placed it on the counter. Then he pulled her into a hug.

She clung to him until he released her.

"You left me in court to berate my brother? You know I never wanted him to find out. I asked you not to come, and you came anyway, and then you just left. I looked up, and you were gone. Why?" she asked, sliding to sit on the floor of the kitchen.

"Because I couldn't just sit there. I listened to all the ways in which that son of a bitch hurt you, and I felt a murderous rage. I wanted to walk up to him right in front of everybody and beat him to a bloody pulp. But I couldn't do it. You wouldn't have appreciated it, and it wouldn't have helped your case," he said, towering over her.

"Then why did you come? I asked you not to come. I didn't want you to hear any of it. I didn't want you to hear how I'd been too weak to leave even at the expense of my life, or how I had put my son in danger. That's not who I am now, and I never wanted you to know about that person."

"You think I would ever consider you weak? After everything you had endured? After you picked yourself up from all that? You are the strongest person I know. I came because I couldn't stay away. I came because I love you. I'm in love with you, Makena. And I want to be there for you, always. I'm sorry that I left because it made you doubt me, doubt my commitment to you."

He held out his hand to her and pulled her up, then to him. He kissed her passionately.

"You've never told me you love me before today. My brother shouldn't have heard it before me. You shouldn't have called him," she said, caressing his cheek.

"You shut me out. You didn't want me in court, you didn't tell me how bad things were with Paul, and you compartmentalized—you and me on one end, and your life on the other. I made space for you in my life, and if Paul hadn't shown up, you probably wouldn't be here. I have been clear about what I want, but I'm not sure about you. Calling Charlie was what I did because I'm not sure about how to talk to you or when the right time to do that is."

"I'm sorry that I ever made you feel that way. You're in my life, all of it. I'm in love with you, I have been for a long time. We need to communicate better from now on, and you can't talk to my brother about me again."

"He was shocked. He had no idea about any of it. You need to talk to him soon and confront him about whatever anger you hold over him. He hasn't been much of a brother to you, but maybe that's because you didn't give him the chance to be." He held her face and kissed her again. "And I will talk to him about you again because I want to ask for your hand in marriage soon, and I'd prefer it if you were getting along when I do."

"Fine, I will talk to him later if you stop talking about him and take me to bed," she said. She stood on tiptoes and kissed him.

"Aren't you due back in court? Not that I'm not looking forward to having you stretched out naked in bed."

"Caitlin will call me if I'm needed. My testimony is over."

She stalked to the bedroom, unbuttoning her blouse. Once inside, she dropped it. She felt David behind her unzipping her skirt and gently pulling it down. She stepped out of it and stood in front of him in just her underwear. His eyes lit up with promise as he laid her on the bed then undressed and joined her. He made love to her gently, and she cried out his name as an orgasm ripped through her.

Much later, they dressed and went to the living room. She had left her phone in her purse by the door, and it had several missed calls from Caitlin. Her heart stopped as she called her back.

"Caitlin, hi. I got your missed call."

"Hi, Makena. I know you're worried, so I'll cut to the chase. Paul didn't want to testify so he agreed to drop the case. He will be signing an affidavit relinquishing his parental rights and giving you Gerald's birth certificate if you agree not to sue him for assault."

Her heart swelled with joy. She squealed, startling David who was in the kitchen making them coffee.

"What happened?" he asked.

"Paul caved. He's dropping the case. It's over."

David lifted her off the ground and swung her around. She laughed in pure, unbridled joy.

Chapter Eighteen

In the weeks that followed, David didn't mention marriage again. Makena concluded he must have decided it was too soon. Everything with them had been a marathon. They had started sleeping together, and then as soon as they decided to start dating, they started living together. All this had taken place within six months. Maybe marriage was where he decided to put the brakes on.

She had called her brother, and they'd had a lengthy talk. He was upset she had been through hell for years and hadn't trusted him to be there for her. While her first instinct would have been to console him, she used the tools she had learned in therapy to be honest with him. She pointed out how he hadn't given her enough reason to trust him. At the end of the call, they'd both felt much better about their relationship. He'd promised to plan a visit as soon as he could. Since then, they'd had weekly phone calls.

The entire court case seemed like a fever dream. Paul had signed an affidavit relinquishing his parental rights over Gerald, and Gerald's birth certificate along with Makena's documents had been delivered to Caitlin's office.

"If it weren't for the fact that you no longer have to worry about him trying to take your son, I would be disappointed by this whole episode. I'm a good lawyer, great at what I do. But that was the silliest case I have ever been a part of. Paul's lawyer is good, but you wouldn't know it from that case. It was like they weren't bothered with winning, which begs the question of why bother dragging you to court?" Caitlin asked.

They were on a girls' night out with Julia and Allison. They had just ordered a bunch of cocktails with Julia ordering a virgin margarita since she was still breastfeeding.

"Honestly, I wondered about it, too, but I don't care. I have everything I ever wanted," Makena said, feeling thankful about how everything had turned out.

The lack of a ring from David didn't bother her that much because their relationship was great. One of the things bothering her, though, was the feeling that they weren't on equal footing since she had needed him and didn't feel as if he needed her. The past months had proven to her how theirs was an enduring love and there wasn't a scale on the level of need.

Allison had suggested the ladies meet up to celebrate her.

"Can we not talk about that bastard? I, for one, am happy to see the back of him," Julia said, and everyone raised their glasses to that.

For the rest of the night, they drank and talked about what had been going on in each other's lives.

David picked her up just past midnight. Julia was okay to drive herself, and Caitlin went with Allison when her husband picked her up. When she got to bed, she quickly fell asleep, thankful it was Saturday.

They had a late morning on Sunday and stayed in bed for hours. They heard Gerald wake up, and since he didn't knock on their door, they stayed put. They hadn't made any plans for the day and were just going to wing it. Find a nice restaurant for lunch and somewhere for Gerald to play. At least, it's what she thought was the plan.

"I want to show you something later after we have lunch," David said.

"Really? I'm curious. Will you tell me what it is?"

She propped herself up to face him. He shook his head, and she ran her hand around his jaw which was sporting a five o'clock shadow.

"I won't. And since you seem all better from last night's partying, I have something else in mind."

He pulled her close and kissed her thoroughly. In no time, they had shed their scarce nightwear. They made love for what seemed like hours. They emerged from the bedroom sometime later, freshly showered.

Makena made a light breakfast since lunch was just a couple of hours away. They settled in front of the TV and let Gerald pick something to watch.

Their Sunday routine was usually relaxed unless they had plans. Usually, it involved visiting family and friends or hosting. They had hosted a small group the previous weekend consisting of David's mother, Allison and her husband and kids, and Julia, Henry, and Lily. Makena had enjoyed cooking for everyone, rejecting David's offer to call a caterer. When lunch was over, they'd gone to the rooftop where the kids had enjoyed swimming and the adults had chatted. They hadn't left until late at night.

A month earlier, she had finalized the sale of her parents' land. Fortunately, with Julia's parents' help, they'd found a buyer from the same area, a young couple. Makena had gone with Gerald and David to meet the buyers. She'd also wanted David to meet Julia's parents and for them to see she and Gerald were well. They had been thrilled with David and made him promise to keep taking good care of them. Makena had assured them he was a great guy.

For the first time in years, she got to visit her parents' grave. She brought flowers and laid them on the headstone which had both their names written on it. She cried at the thought of saying goodbye to her entire past. Although she hadn't lived there in almost a decade, she had held onto it as a talisman of her childhood, the last place where she felt safe. But it was time to let go, and she had another safe space now. The buyers assured her she could visit the graves whenever she wanted. She knew she would be taking them up on their offer.

Charlie had insisted she keep his share of the money from the sale, but she was reluctant. So he'd asked her to open an account for Gerald in case he ever needed it. That didn't go over well with David who insisted he could provide for Gerald. Still, Makena opened the account and thanked her brother. Having lived the life she had, she knew that things changed, people changed, parents died. If anything happened to her, this would be a nice nest egg for her son, one she'd never had.

In the afternoon, they drove to a restaurant along Mombasa Road for lunch. The place had a children's park so they let Gerald play for a while before they left.

"You better not be getting us a dog. I don't want one, no matter how much Gerald begs," she said, trying to get the surprise out of him.

"No dog, and stop trying to get it out of me. It's a surprise."

"I don't do well with surprises, you know that."

"I promise you, this will be good. Sometimes, when someone surprises you, it's because they love you very much," he said, then reached across the table for her hand. She was wearing the watch he'd given her, a favourite of hers. He had added to her jewellery collection with a pair of gold earrings on Valentine's Day.

"Okay, but don't forget that tomorrow is Monday," she added.

He chuckled. "I would call you a spoilsport, but I don't think that would be in my best interest. Don't worry, I will get us home on time."

She sighed in contentment.

An hour later, they were back on the road, this time headed along Thika Road. They took an exit that led them to an estate with gorgeous mansions. David stopped the car in a vacant piece of land surrounded by a barbed wire fence and an open gate. There was a small white tent in the middle with a table and four plastic chairs. An older man approached them. David lowered the car window.

"*Habari yako Bwana David*," he greeted in Swahili.

David shook his hand.

"Hello, Kamau. This is Makena and Gerald," he introduced them.

Makena shook the man's hand, and Gerald nodded and waved from the back of the car.

"I've finished setting up. Call me before you leave," he said and walked off.

David drove in through the gate and parked the car. He opened the door and then quickly walked around to open her door and held out his hand for her.

She got a good look around. The land was large and a distance from the other houses in the estate. On the table under the tent, there was a bunch of lilies.

"Look around and let me know what you think," David said, releasing her hand.

She walked around admiring the newly planted grass. She noticed David had left her side and been replaced by Gerald. He was standing inside the tent opening a bottle of wine. She went to him and placed a hand on his back.

"This is lovely. Whose is it?"

"I'm glad you like it. It's ours. I want us to build our house here, but only if you like it enough," he said then handed her a glass of wine. He poured Gerald a glass of orange juice and handed it to him.

"I love it," she said, excited at the prospect. She kissed his cheek. "When did you buy it?"

"I bought it years ago with part of my inheritance as an investment. But now, I think it's a wonderful place for us to build our home and raise our children. All ten of them."

She laughed.

"Just as soon as they figure out a way for men to go through pregnancy. Two more, at most," she countered.

David shrugged. "We'll see." He set his glass down on the table and took hers. "I have something else for you."

He handed her the bunch of pink lilies. There was a velvet black box in the middle, and she just knew. She felt her heart beat faster and a sheen of tears cover her eyes, blurring her vision as she took out the box and opened it. It contained a silver engagement ring with a large pink diamond centre surrounded by smaller clear diamonds on either side. She put the flowers on the table and took the ring out of the box. In front of her, David was on one knee.

"In my mind and my heart, you are already my wife. I can't imagine growing old without you, and I don't want to. Here, where we will build our home, in Gerald's presence, this is where our story begins. Will you marry me?"

Makena ran her hands across her teary eyes, and in the process, she dropped the ring. David picked it up and held it out. She stretched out her hand.

"You didn't answer, Mum," Gerald said.

She laughed amidst the tears. "Yes, I will marry you, David."

He slipped the ring on her finger, and it fit like a glove. He kissed it and released her hand. She held it out for Gerald to see.

"I have something for you, too, Gerald." He handed him a larger box which he opened to reveal a watch. "Now that your mum and I are getting married, if you want, you can call me Dad, because I will be your father. I will take care of you and your mum."

His words were simple, but Makena knew how heavy they were in their implication. David had warned her against referring to Gerald as "baggage" long before they had gotten together. He had bonded with him before she even knew she loved him. He had made room for him in his house, his life, his family, and most importantly, in his heart. This was the most natural transition. She was touched he'd asked Gerald rather than demanded or imposed. She was even more touched that he had included him in the proposal.

Gerald simply nodded, but he went in for a hug. She pulled out her phone and snapped a quick photo of the moment. When they pulled her in the hug, she faced David and mouthed "thank you." And for once, when they kissed as Gerald looked up at them, he didn't make a sound.

THE NEXT DAY, AT WORK, Makena couldn't stop staring at the ring. Everyone congratulated her on the engagement as soon as they noticed the ring. When she called Julia on the drive home to inform her, she didn't sound surprised. She had helped David pick the ring. His sister and mum were not surprised, either, when he called them. While they hadn't been in on the plan, they said they knew it was happening sooner rather than later.

Makena was so blissful in her joy that when a niggling feeling started creeping up later in the day, she ignored it. She didn't even think much of it when her phone rang. But when caller ID revealed it was Gerald's school, she decided it was time to worry. They had never called her.

"Hello, Mama Gerald, this is the principal at your son's school. Something has happened."

She sat up straight. "What happened? Is my son okay?"

"Yes, I think he's okay. His father came and took him. He was accompanied by police officers and had a birth certificate that showed he is the father. We requested he wait for you, but he said that you were keeping his son from him. Gerald seemed scared of him, and he was crying. They had a GK car and threatened to arrest anyone who tried to stop them."

Makena grabbed her bag and headed for the door, struggling to keep the phone on her ear.

"How long ago did this happen?" She took a deep breath and tried to remain calm enough to get the details.

"They just drove out of the gate a minute ago. I took the number plates for the car. Do you want me to call the police?" the principal asked.

"I'll call them. I'm on my way." She hung up and called David.

He picked up after the first ring.

"Hello, future wife. Miss me already?" he started.

She cut him short. "Paul took Gerald from school."

"I'll pick you up, wait for me inside the office gate. Don't come out. He could be coming for you next."

She took his advice. But she didn't care if he took her if that meant she could be with her son. David arrived ten minutes later. It was in the middle of the day, and there was no traffic, which helped because it took them less than twenty minutes to get to the school. In the car, he tried to assure her that her son would be fine.

"He is his father. I don't think he would hurt him," he said.

"You don't know what he is capable of," she responded quietly.

He held her hand and felt the slight tremble.

"We'll do whatever it takes to bring our son home. If it's money he wants, then we'll give it to him."

"He doesn't want money," she said with resignation.

The only thing Paul wanted was control. He had lulled her into a false sense of security by pretending to leave them alone.

He dropped the lawsuit, signed away his rights, and when they were relaxed, he swooped in to ruin it all.

At the school, the principal didn't have any more details about the situation beyond the car's number plates. She said there had been two officers aside from Paul, all in uniform and with guns. Since the school's security wasn't armed, she hadn't wanted to risk the safety of the other students.

Makena tried calling Paul using the last number he had contacted her with, but his phone was switched off. She tried all the other numbers. Then she called his parents who said they hadn't seen him in over a month.

When they got to the police station, they learnt that the car Paul used was from a police station in Kiambu County and had been in the garage for servicing and wasn't assigned to anyone. They also learnt Paul was on leave. When his wife was contacted by the station, she said she'd left him immediately after the court case. She had been put on unpaid leave for covering for Paul in court. Since they were living in her house, she'd kicked him out and didn't know where he'd ended up. They were also told Gerald couldn't be listed as a missing person because it was too soon—they had to wait at least twenty-four hours.

By the time they drove home, drained and frustrated, they had no idea where Gerald was or what Paul wanted. They had reached out to Caitlin who was in contact with Paul's lawyer, but she hadn't heard anything, either. They spent the night on the phone trying to get whatever information they could, but nothing was useful.

Chapter Nineteen

After a restless night, Makena woke up at five a.m. and shook David awake.

"We need to go to Paul's parents' home. They have to know where he is. I want them to look me in the face and lie to me."

"Okay, let's go," he said after a slight hesitation.

They drove the two-hour drive in silence aside from the occasional calls she made to her office letting them know about the crisis she was dealing with and their family and friends. She also texted Charlie who would probably be asleep due to the time difference.

She had barely cried, but her eyes were red and swollen from the lack of sleep. She had promised herself she would do whatever it took to get her son back, and crying wouldn't help. She directed David to the home of Paul's parents, a mansion on the outskirts of Naivasha town. He honked, and when the gateman saw her, he opened the gate. It was just after seven a.m., and the compound was quiet.

Before they even got out of the car, the door opened, and both of Paul's parents stepped out. His mother was still in her nightdress with a leso wrapped around her waist and a headscarf on her head. She let out a yawn and rubbed her eyes.

"Makena, what are you doing here this early in the morning?"

Makena looked at her strangely, surprised she was refusing to acknowledge her call the previous evening informing her Paul had kidnapped Gerald.

"Paul kidnapped Gerald from school yesterday, I told you that. You must know where he is, tell me. I just want my son back."

"Kidnapped him? Why would he kidnap his son? He didn't kidnap him. He took him, just like you did five years ago. You kept our grandson away from us for five years," Paul's mother said, edging close to Makena. She stopped right in front of her. Makena looked to Paul's father who was leaning against a pillar nonchalantly. "I don't know where he is, but Paul loves his son. He will be fine."

"Please, Mama Paul, I'm begging you. He beat us, that's why I left with Gerald. He broke his hand, and I lost my other baby. I just want my son to be safe," she pleaded, her eyes filling with tears.

"That was an accident, and you humiliated him in court for it. Don't worry, I can see you're about to get married. You will get more children if Paul decides to keep Gerald."

Makena dropped to her knees and clasped her hands.

"Please," she wailed. "Please tell me where my son is."

Paul's mother turned her back to her and started walking to the door. Makena crawled after her, and she pushed her away. She landed painfully on her back. David, who had been watching the exchange silently, rushed to her side and held her. She sobbed into his chest. Paul's father joined them and squatted next to her.

"Are you okay?" he asked.

"I just want my son back," she whispered, raising her head.

"She's telling the truth. He hasn't called us, and he isn't picking up our calls. Maybe you can try his wife. I'll send you the location of her house. They weren't living together when we spoke last, but maybe she knows more than we do. If he reaches out, I'll contact you. I don't want any harm to come to my grandson, either."

David helped Makena up, and they waited while Paul's father sent her the location of Paul's wife's house. They got back in the car, and as they drove off, she saw the look of disdain on Paul's mother's face.

"What kind of mother just stands by as her child does despicable things? I know she never liked me, but to watch this happen and not do anything? She knew all along that her son was a monster."

She pulled several tissues from the box and wiped her eyes. The drive to Rachel's house was about thirty minutes. She wanted to be calm and collected by the time they got there.

She handed her phone to David to follow the map to the location they were given. Forty minutes later, they stopped outside a bungalow. They got out of the car and rang the bell.

Rachel opened the small gate five minutes later looking heavily pregnant.

"What are you doing here, Makena? I told you I don't know where Paul is."

This time, David interjected. "May we come in?"

Rachel hesitated.

"You think I'm hiding him here? Why would I do that? He's a monster."

"And yet, you testified for him in court," Makena said snarkily. "I'm sorry, I shouldn't have said that. All I want is to find my son."

"You can come in if you want, but I assure you he's not here," Rachel said, stepping aside.

Makena looked at David hesitantly, and he nodded. They walked inside. Rachel led them inside the house into the sitting room. She was surprised to see a wedding photo of Rachel and Paul on the wall. Paul in his blue uniform and Rachel in a white strapless gown staring intimately into his eyes. He had his hand at the small of her back, and she had hers up on the back of his neck. They held each other close. Rachel noticed her looking at it.

"I haven't gotten around to removing that." She gestured for them to sit. "Do you want some tea?"

She started to head for the kitchen, but Makena stopped her, letting her know they wouldn't be long.

"Do you know where Paul could have gone? Or any friends of his who may be helping him?"

Rachel sighed. "Paul doesn't have friends. He has people he uses to do his bidding. When they become disposable, he drops them. None of our colleagues speaks to him anymore. When you called last night, I called everyone I knew who could have helped him, but there is no one."

She paused for a breath then continued "What happened in court was a wakeup call for me. I had buried my head in the sand about what kind of man I married for years. But hearing what he did to you, knowing he would do it to me eventually, I couldn't stay with him. He had already started beating me, and he was cheating on me. I was ashamed to admit to myself after what I had allowed to happen to you, but you were brave, even when you had no one or nothing. Fortunately, I had the means to protect myself. I reached out to a journalist, Pauline Ngige. I will be telling her my story. I won't cover up anything. I don't want any other woman to suffer at Paul's hands. If Gerald won't have been found yet, we can ask her for help."

"Thank you," Makena said, recognising how genuine Rachel was being. She stood up to leave and begged Rachel to call her if she heard from Paul.

That afternoon, they stopped by the police station again and were told nothing had been heard. At Caitlin's suggestion, Makena wrote an appeal on Facebook. She had to create a new account because she had never joined. She shared a recent photo of Gerald at the school skating field holding his helmet and giving her that adorable grin of his. She also shared a photo of Paul she got from Rachel. She explained her situation with Paul and shared her, David's, and Caitlin's phone numbers so that if anyone spotted him or Paul, they could call them or report them to the police. Everyone in their circle shared it on social media, and a lot of people commented, empathizing with her. But no one had any information.

Later that evening, Mrs. Mutua came to visit with them. She brought them food, and even though she hadn't eaten since the previous day, Makena could barely touch it.

"You need to eat," Mrs. Mutua insisted, sitting next to her.

"I'm not hungry."

"Try, even if you aren't. How are you going to find your son if you're weak? Please, eat something," she said gently.

Makena forced herself to eat several spoonful and drank a glass of milk which Mrs. Mutua had insisted would help her sleep.

"What if we never find him? Not even Paul's parents know where he is," she asked, allowing herself to consider that possibility for the first time. A whole day had passed, and Paul hadn't done anything; he hadn't called or texted. What if he intended to keep Gerald forever, out of some morbid sense of entitlement since she had done the same?

"We will do whatever it takes to bring him back. Tomorrow, I will send a private investigator who will help you. If the police are not doing their jobs, then we will do it," Mrs. Mutua said.

"Thank you, Mum. We really appreciate it," David said.

"He is my grandson, too. There's no need to thank me."

She sat with them for a couple of hours and even prayed with them. Then when David started to notice she was getting tired, he called her driver to take her home.

IN BED, DAVID HELD Makena close as she was wracked with sobs.

"If anything happens to Gerald, I won't survive it."

She had let her guard down, allowed herself to relax and think Paul had become a sane, reasonable person. If this cost her her son, she couldn't deal. No wonder he had been so unbothered in court. He had no plan of letting her keep her son.

"Don't worry, we'll find him," David said, and he kissed her forehead.

As if it was easy not to worry. Worry wasn't a button she could switch off whenever she wanted. Maybe it was easy for him because Gerald wasn't his son. She immediately blocked that thought—it was unfair to think of him this way because two days earlier, he'd promised them he would be his father. Even before that, he had taken on the role of his father whole-heartedly.

Eventually, she heard him snore softly, an indication he had fallen asleep. Unable to do the same, she rolled off the bed and quietly walked out of the room. She opened the door to her son's room for the first time since he was taken.

It was just as Gerald had left it the previous day. The bed was haphazardly made, and books and pens were on the study table. She hadn't had time to straighten it because she'd been running late for work. She straightened it and pulled back the covers and slipped inside. She placed her phone beside the pillow and closed her eyes. It took hours to fall asleep.

It seemed like minutes later when her phone rang. She quickly sat up and checked the time—just after five a.m. The phone rang again, and she remembered what had woken her up. She answered it.

"Hello, my love."

She quickly turned the lights on and stood up.

"Paul, where is my son?"

"He's with me. Don't worry, he's fine," he said nonchalantly.

She counted to five to calm herself down. She knew she had to try not to agitate him.

"I just want to know whether he's okay. Please let me talk to him."

"He's asleep. I won't wake him up just to satisfy your curiosity. Besides, you'll see him soon enough."

"When will I see him? Where are you?" she asked, pacing up and down the room.

"I'm sending you a car. It will be there in fifteen minutes. If you tell anyone, this will be the last you hear from me, and you will never see our son again." He hung up.

Makena took off her engagement ring and placed it on the desk. Then, she took out a pen and paper and wrote a note to David. There was so much she wanted to tell him, but she couldn't. She didn't even know where she was going, and even if she did, she couldn't tell him and endanger her son. Instead, she wrote simply.

David, I have to go find my son.

Please hold onto this for me, I'll be back.

I love you

Yours, Makena

She placed the ring and the note on the coffee table and slipped out quietly. She didn't even change because all her clothes were in her bedroom, and she didn't want to risk waking David up. She was dressed in a T-shirt and sweatpants and a jacket she had grabbed from the laundry basket outside the bedroom.

She opened the gate and walked out. According to the watch, she had less than two minutes left. There was no car in sight. Five minutes later, just as she was about to call Paul, the police car they had taken to Gerald's school arrived. She didn't recognise the driver.

"Makena?" he asked.

She nodded.

He signalled for her to get in. A few kilometres away from the house, he asked for her phone and threw it out of the window onto the road. Then he called Paul and let him know they were on the way.

Chapter Twenty

They drove for almost an hour. Nairobi was just waking up, and there were barely any shops open. The lights were still on in the city and its outskirts. The roads were clear of the traffic jams she knew would cover them as morning came.

Their solitary car cruised through Limuru, one of the coldest parts of the country. The vehicle stopped just past vast tea plantations, after driving from the tarmacked road onto a dirt track for several minutes. They were outside a brown gate surrounded by an incomplete stone fence.

The man in the driver's seat asked her to get out of the car and get inside the gate. She did as she was told, hoping against hope that her son was inside, but scared of what Paul might have done to him. She pushed the gate open and had barely taken a step inside when she was pulled through.

"Makena, my love. Thanks for coming," Paul said, pulling her into a hug.

She stood still, stiff as a board, and tried not to flinch. He let her go and locked the gate.

"Where's Gerald?" she asked, looking around.

There was an incomplete bungalow which had never gone past roofing and had doors and windows without panes installed. It looked like it had been around for a while.

"He's inside. Come on, let me show you our house."

He grabbed her arm painfully and led her to the door. Inside, in what was meant to be the sitting room, there was a single couch. The floor was rough, and the walls had not been plastered. He led her to one of the rooms which had a small bed and a mattress. Gerald lay there covered in a blanket. He sat up as soon as he heard them.

"Mum!" he exclaimed, then he ran to her and hugged her. "Mum, are you going to take me home?"

Makena held him tightly, breathing in his scent, tears brimming in her eyes. Paul tore them apart by pulling Gerald away.

"Your mother is here to stay with us. This is our home now."

Gerald protested, grabbing his mother.

"No, it's not, and you're a bad person. You hurt Mum, and you took me away without asking. You can't force us to stay here."

Paul took a step towards them, and for the first time, she noticed the gun in his hand. A cold sweat ran down her back. She grabbed Gerald and pulled him behind her.

"Shhhhh, Gerald. We're going to be fine. He's not going to hurt us anymore. Are you, Paul?" she asked, looking pointedly at him.

If he had any humanity left, he would see he was agitating the boy. He took a deep breath.

"No, your mum is right, son. I don't want to hurt you."

He slumped on the lone plastic seat in the room, and she led Gerald back to the bed where they sat down.

"Are you hurt? Did he hit you?" she whispered, checking his face and arms.

"He didn't hurt me."

She stood up and went to Paul's side.

"Why are you doing this? You promised that you would leave us alone."

"I promised nothing," he said angrily. "Those were just papers that needed signing. Do you think I went to court because I thought it was a great idea? No, I had to see you standing there, pretending you were a perfect wife. Everything I did, I did for a reason, even leaving you alone for five years."

Shock filled her at the insinuation.

"You think I didn't know where you were every day for the past five years? Just because you kept packing up and moving from place to place? You have no idea the laugh I had watching you panic over and over again. In fact, I would have left you alone if you hadn't decided to whore yourself out to your boss's son," he declared arrogantly.

Makena leaned back against the wall and closed her eyes. She had spent five years on the run, thinking she had escaped him each time. But he'd known where she was. He'd known all along, and he had only come after her when she'd started dating David. He would never let her be happy—he wanted her to be alone forever.

"What do you want from me?" she asked quietly.

Paul stood up and came in front of her. He ran the gun across her chest.

"I want us to be together. You are mine," he said, lowering his voice dangerously.

She saw Gerald watching them closely.

"Then let him go. Let Gerald go, and I will do whatever you want."

Paul backhanded her across the face, and she landed on the rough floor, scrapping her elbow.

"Do you take me for a fool? Why do you think I took him first? I know the minute I let him go, you will never stop fighting me."

She sat down on the floor and pulled her knees to her chest.

"I bought this land for us, and I started building this house for us, only for you to run off because we fought. I was trying to change, and you didn't give me a chance. You pushed me into the arms of that bitch Rachel, and now, she's gone, too. We belong together," he said, getting agitated.

"As long as you're holding my son captive, I won't stop fighting. If you let him go, there are people who can take care of him, and you can keep me. But I won't let him be your prisoner," she stated, looking straight at him.

Paul held his face in his hands and shook his head over and over again. Makena stood up and went back to her son. She hugged him and whispered in his ear.

"When I tell you to run, just do it. Don't look back or stop, run until you're out of here. Can you climb over the fence?" she asked hopefully.

The fence wasn't too high, and the other side was all dirt so even if he fell, he wouldn't be hurt badly. Gerald nodded, and she sighed with relief.

"If you find someone, ask them to call Auntie Julia. Don't try to come back here, just show the police where it is. If I don't come back, I want you to know that I love you, very much. You are the light of my life, and I will be okay because you're safe. Auntie Julia will take care of you, and Uncle David will help. I love you, my angel," she said, tears running down her face.

She kissed his forehead and then left him. She went back to Paul who had returned to his seat. She straddled his lap and hugged him.

"If you let him go, I'll stop fighting you. We can leave and go wherever you want. I just can't be with you if you're keeping him prisoner." She kissed his mouth, feeling disgusted as he shoved his wet tongue into her mouth. "Let him go, okay? Please. Gerald, you can go now, run!"

She held Paul firmly, acting as a shield if he decided to try and shoot Gerald. She would be between her son and any bullet. She heard Gerald shuffle and run past them through the door. She continued kissing Paul, feeling his cold, clammy hands running all over her face. She felt the cold steel of the gun on her back where he'd lifted her shirt.

She felt him pull off her jacket, and she let him. In her head, she was counting the seconds until she knew her son was safe on the other side of the fence. She closed her eyes and shut out everything that was happening. But she still felt him harden between her legs, his clammy hands pawing at her breasts.

When she reached two hundred, she pulled away and looked around. Her son was nowhere to be seen. She heaved a sigh of relief. She stepped away from Paul and straightened her shirt.

"Come back, baby," he said, and when she didn't react, he grabbed her scraped elbow, eliciting a painful yelp from her.

She pushed him back with all her might, catching him unawares. He fell back on his chair and dropped the gun. She reached for it, but he was faster, grabbing it and hitting her in the face with it.

"You stupid bitch. Don't think for a second I won't kill you and find that brat and kill him, too. Sit down."

He pointed the gun at her head, and she sat on the bed. He held her shoulder and punched her in the stomach. She clutched her midsection in pain.

"This is for trying to escape me. I will never let you go, and now that you tricked me into letting the brat go, we have to leave. You are mine, and I will never let you go, and if you try to leave me, I will blow that brat's brains first and then yours, just to teach you a lesson."

Makena knew if they left the house, she was done for—there would be little chance of escaping him. She kneed him in the groin, causing him to double down and land on the floor. He dropped the gun, and this time, she was ready. She grabbed it and aimed it at him.

He picked up a piece of wood and swung it at her. She stepped back, causing him to miss. She had never held a gun before, but she had seen his gun several times. It had been used to terrorise her for years. She aimed it at him and pulled the trigger.

There was a loud bang that almost deafened her, and she felt the kickback in her hand. She thought she had missed because she didn't see where the bullet had hit, but suddenly, there was a red spot on his shoulder, rapidly covering his grey shirt.

Her first feeling was relief that she hadn't killed him. There was a look of shock on his face like he couldn't believe it. The gun still in her hands, she thought back to what he had said. She knew if he lived, he would never stop hunting her. She also knew he wouldn't be in jail long, if at all. He knew where she was at all times; he had kidnapped her son from his school. Even getting custody of Gerald in court meant nothing.

She couldn't live like that one more day, terrified of what he would do to them. He'd threatened to kill her son. As long as he was alive, Gerald would never be safe, she would never stop looking over her shoulder, and if he took Gerald again, her boy wouldn't survive.

Paul raised his hands in surrender, noticing her finger still on the trigger. She closed her eyes and let the tears flow freely. Then she opened them, aimed the gun at his head, and pulled the trigger.

Immediately after, she heard a gasp from the doorway. She turned around to look, but not before she saw Paul hit the ground with a hole in his forehead. David quickly strode from the door to her side.

"The police are on their way. You have to tell them that he wouldn't stop coming at you even after you shot him in the shoulder," he whispered.

She dropped the gun and embraced him.

"He wasn't going to stop."

He held her as she started shaking uncontrollably. He lifted her and carried her out of the door and through the gate and to his waiting car. Just then, the police arrived. Makena heard him tell them Paul was dead and he was taking her to the hospital. They tried to insist on talking to her first, but she was still shaking. He told them which hospital he was taking her to and set her in the car. He got in the driver's seat and pulled away.

Makena drifted away.

When she came to, she was on a hospital bed covered with a thin blanket. She felt a throbbing headache. She heard voices from outside.

"We have to talk to her now. Paul's parents are asking what happened to their son, and you're blocking the door from the only person who can tell us," someone said.

"She still hasn't awoken, and I won't allow you to interfere with her healing process."

It was Dr. Shikuku. They had brought her right back where it started. She tried to pull herself to sit up, but her hand was in pain.

"This wouldn't have happened if you had done your job in the first place. Paul's history of abuse is well documented, and you didn't do anything to protect Makena, even when she came to you. It took a PI and me one hour to find him, and you had shit for two days while he held her son captive. If you try to victimize her, I will insist that you wait for her lawyer before speaking to her," David said.

When he peered through the door and saw her awake, he rushed to her side.

"David," she whispered.

He joined her on the bed and held her hand. Dr Shikuku and two police officers joined them.

"We have to stop meeting like this, Makena. How are you feeling?" she asked.

"I have a headache, and my arm hurts. Where is Gerald?"

"He's home with my mum. He's fine. We found him on the road trying to get help. He's a very brave boy," David said.

"Madam, we have some questions for you about what happened."

David started to protest, but she said she would talk to them. She told them what had happened, telling them she had shot Paul because he kept coming at her with the piece of wood. She left out the part about him dropping it when she shot his shoulder.

"Thank you, madam. That will be all for now. We'll call you if we have any more questions."

She nodded, and they left.

"Thank you for finding me," she said to David as she laid her head on his shoulder.

"I had to. You left your ring." He reached into his pocket and pulled out the ring, then put it on her finger. "Don't take it off again."

"I won't," she promised.

"The doctor said I can take you home. There's a whole lot of people waiting to see you, but I can send them all away if you don't feel up to it," he said, caressing the finger he had just put the ring on.

"It's okay, I don't mind. I want to see everyone. I thought I was going to die and you'd have to take care of Gerald. I told him Julia would. I didn't want you to have to do it alone."

David held her, and she cried. She was angry at herself for crying—she felt like it was all she had done the past two days. She shuddered at the thought that she had killed Paul.

"David, I killed someone," she whispered.

"You did what you had to do, and if you hadn't, I would have," he said quietly. "But Makena, you can't tell anyone. He attacked you, and you defended yourself, that's all."

He held her for several minutes until she pulled away.

"I want to go home. I don't want to be here," she said.

He helped her up. Her clothes were dirty and torn, but she had no choice but to wear them. David settled the bill and got her prescribed painkillers, and they left.

At home, they were met with a chaotic scene. It seemed like everyone was there. Julia and Lily, Caitlin, Allison and her children, and David's mum. But the biggest surprise was when just as Makena settled on the couch, her brother emerged from the kitchen.

"Hey, sis," he greeted cheerfully.

She tried to stand up cautiously, but Charlie went to her and hugged her where she sat. For a minute, she was lost for words.

"What are you doing here? When did you get here?" she asked.

"My nephew was kidnapped. Of course I had to come. And if Paul wasn't dead already, I would have killed him."

She looked around for Gerald, worried he might have heard, but the children were no longer in the room. She wanted to tell him about Paul's death herself.

"You'd have had to get in line," David stated.

She saw how serious he was.

"Are you okay?" Charlie asked.

"Yeah, it's bumps and bruises, but they'll heal. My son is safe, that's what matters."

"I wouldn't have been okay with you dying, Makena. I know I'm not up for bro of the year, but I love you. What you did, going without telling anybody, was crazy and dangerous."

"I had no choice," she said matter of factly.

"You're both safe now, that's what matters. And as soon as the bumps and bruises are healed, we can talk about wedding planning. How many goats are you taking to get her off your hands?" Julia asked Charlie.

He chuckled.

"There will be no goats because I am not property, will there, Charlie?"

He shook his head and raised his hands. They all laughed.

She looked at them, her family, both by blood and by love, and her heart filled with love for them. Now, she just had to check on her son, and she would be at peace. She could hear him with Gianna and Nathan in his bedroom, but she had to see him and hug him.

Epilogue

our Years Later

Makena looked at her reflection in the mirror in the entryway console and smiled, proud of the woman who looked back at her. She couldn't believe how much had happened in so little time. She took a step back and bumped into her husband.

"Careful," he said as he steered her back inside their house. He placed her on one of the recliner couches and sat next to her.

"Can I take it off now? It's so hot," she complained.

"No, I'm the one who gets to take it off. That's my present. Here's yours," he said, handing her a folder.

"Only you can make a graduation gown sound sexy," she said with a laugh. "And you didn't need to give me anything. I have everything I could ever want."

"You're going to love this. Open it," he said eagerly.

Makena opened the folder. There was a logo emblazoned with Furaha Foundation at the top of the first page. She read through the page. It was an appointment letter for her to run the foundation. The next pages included registration with the national NGO body and office addresses. There was also a deed for a safe house.

"When did you do this? How?" she asked.

"Over the past few months. I wanted to surprise you. I know this is what you've always wanted to do, help people. And now, you have the knowledge and the means to do so."

She threw her arms around him. "Thank you. I don't know what to say. This is amazing."

He hugged her tight. She was awed with gratitude. This was what she wanted to do with her life. She wanted to create a community for helping women who had been through the same thing she had.

It had taken years of therapy to come to terms with what she had done, especially when she'd had to get help without actually saying what she was getting help for. The day she came home from the hospital after everyone left, she'd sat Gerald down and told him Paul was dead. Then, she had gotten him into therapy, too, determined to get him all the help he needed to cope. Paul's father had reached out to apologize for what Paul had done months after his death. Eventually, Makena had forgiven herself.

She and David got married months later, and their identical twin daughters, named after his mum and hers, had come soon after. They were their little honeymoon babies. They had arrived just in time to move into their new house. Now, at almost three years, they were running them ragged, but they wouldn't have it any other way.

"You're happy?" he asked.

"Blissfully so. If I was any happier, I would burst. Just for this, I will keep the gown on," she said with a wink.

"What are you planning? I can see it in that devilish grin," he said with a chuckle.

"Nothing you won't like," she said and pulled him into a passionate kiss.

He deepened the kiss and went to undo her gown. Her breathing quickened as his hand started to slip into the front of her pink V-neck bodycon dress.

"Do we have time?" he asked, eyeing the stairs.

Before she could answer, they heard tiny footsteps run into the house and quickly separated.

"Mummy, Bella took Lily's candy," their older twin Cece called out.

David sighed in disappointment, then they both laughed. They weren't surprised Cece was snitching—the twins could be a team or foes, depending on the day. It seemed today, they were foes.

"Where is Gerald?" David asked.

At thirteen, he was the twins' favourite person. He was thrilled when they were born and had tried to learn how to hold both of them at the same time. David had stepped in and told him to wait until they could walk then he could hold each in one hand. They loved him even more than they loved their parents. When they were at war, he was able to calm them down and get them to make up.

Cece shrugged, indicating she had no idea where her brother was. They wouldn't be surprised if he was showing off the rabbit hatch he had insisted they build him in the backyard. A neighbour had given him two rabbits, and he'd taken them immediately. Caring for them was his favourite pastime.

"I'll deal with this. You can come out when you're ready," David said.

He took Cece's hand, and she led him to where the scuffle was taking place.

Makena looked through the papers David had given her again. He had put in a lot of work because everything was in place. She couldn't wait to get started. She placed the papers in the drawer on the coffee table and locked it. She had learnt to keep important things under lock and key because the twins' hobby was shredding things with their teeth. She took another glance in the mirror. She was none the worse for wear after her passionate incident with David. She put on her graduation cap and stepped out.

Outside on the lush green grass was a tent with several seats. Their guests had already arrived. Her sister-in-law and her family, Julia, heavily pregnant with her second child, Charlie and his fiancée, Caitlin and her husband, David's mum, and a few of their other friends and neighbours.

As she walked towards the tent, everyone stood and clapped. Bella ran to her, and she stretched out her hand for her. David joined them with Cece clutching his hand, and he held out his other hand for her. Gerald joined them, taking Cece's other hand, and they walked to the front of the group, the exact spot where David had proposed years earlier. Makena's heart swelled with love and pride at the family they had built.

"Dad, the rabbit gave birth," Gerald whispered to David.

"Well, are you ready for the babies?"

"Yes, and they're called kittens," Gerald said.

Makena groaned. Gerald was going to boarding school in two months, and she would be left to fend for the kits. She

wasn't fully signed up for the idea of boarding school or rabbits.

The End

Thank you for reading Fugitive Heart by Mathitu Wairimu. If you enjoyed this book, support the author by writing a brief review on the site of purchase.

Find out more about upcoming book releases by the author, sign up for our newsletter at

https://www.loveafricapress.com/newsletter

About the author

Mathitu Wairimu is a Kenyan writer, born and raised in a small village near Nairobi. She has a Bachelor's degree in Education (English and Literature). She spends her time writing and working as a freelance web designer. She fell in love with reading and writing from a young age. Her introduction to romance novels was Mills and Boon, when she was in high school. She longed for love stories that featured characters and places she could relate to, and this inspired her to write such stories. This is her debut novel.

Social media

Facebook: https://www.facebook.com/mathitu.wairimu/

Instagram: https://www.instagram.com/mathituwrites?

Twitter: https://x.com/mathitu_wairimu?

Tiktok: https://www.tiktok.com/@mathituwairimu

Other books by Love Africa Press

Love Prey by Tidimalo Motukwa
Like Whirlwind by Feyi Aina
Trophy Wife by Kiru Taye
Sweetest Fortune by Bambo Deen
CONNECT WITH US
Facebook.com/LoveAfricaPress[1]
Twitter.com/LoveAfricaPress[2]
Instagram.com/LoveAfricaPress[3]
Threads.com/LoveAfricaPress[4]
SIGN UP TO OUR NEWSLETTER
https://www.loveafricapress.com/newsletter

1. https://www.facebook.com/LoveAfricaPress

2. https://twitter.com/LoveAfricaPress

3. https://www.instagram.com/loveafricapress/

4. https://www.threads.net/@loveafricapress